HER *FLAW*SOME LIFE

BY L.A. DONAHOE

I wanted to keep reading HER FLAWSOME LIFE because I couldn't wait to find out what happened next! Loved it! The characters were very relatable.

SHARON D.

Thoroughly enjoyed HER FLAWSOME LIFE! It was very funny and I loved it! I especially liked François! He was hilarious!

GILLIAN W.

I really enjoyed reading HER FLAWSOME LIFE! I found the story fun and the characters entertaining.

LYNDA C.

A wonderful story of a young woman reconciling her past in order to embrace her future. Enjoyable from start to finish.

ANTJE R.

HER
*FLAW*SOME
LIFE

L.A. DONAHOE

www.firstchoicebooks.ca
Victoria, BC

L.A. Donahoe

COVER IMAGES:
Dandelion vector by lupulluss, www.shutterstock.com (Image ID: 292913603)
Silhouette by MikeDotta, www.shutterstock.com (Image ID: 563555992)

Cover and layout design by Jenny Engwer, *First Choice Books*

Author photo by Montse Alvarado, *Beautiful Images by Montserrat, Campbellford, Ontario*

Issued in print and electronic formats.

ISBN: 978-0-2285-0119-0 (paperback)
ISBN: 978-0-2285-0219-7 (html)

Printed in Canada ♻ on recycled paper

FIRST CHOICE BOOKS

firstchoicebooks.ca
Victoria, BC

10 9 8 7 6 5 4 3 2 1

Pursuing my dream...

Thank you to my son, Josh, family and friends for your support and encouragement while I pursue this crazy dream of mine and a special thank you to the following:

A.J. Bonner

L. Clarke

P.J. Donahoe

S. Donahoe

A. Reid

G. "Bean" Warford

NOVELS BY L.A. DONAHOE
JUST THEIR LUCK

Finished reading JUST THEIR LUCK last night. I thought I had predicted the ending, but boy was I wrong! It was the perfect book to relax with. Well done, L.A. Donahoe. I look forward to your next book.

· · · · · ·

This is a very engaging story with fun, interesting characters and a great storyline. I was disappointed when it ended.

· · · · · ·

This storyline kept me wanting to read more, hated that I had to stop to go to work! But I found the story moving, funny, exciting and a little suspenseful. Can't wait for your next book!

· · · · · ·

This is a joyful read! Easily the best rainy Sunday read of the year! The author has captured the characters personalities so well, I could almost hear them speaking in their respective voices! Can't wait for her next book!!

· · · · · ·

Great book. Couldn't wait to find out what was going to happen next. Congratulations!

· · · · · ·

For her first attempt at writing a novel, L.A. Donahoe has developed a plot and characters that keep the reader interested and involved. The story line is humorous at times, depicting people and their activities in small town life.

· · · · · ·

JUST THEIR LUCK was fun, entertaining and a perfect end-of-summer read. It made me smile and I was always waiting for Travis to show up. WELL DONE!

ONE

*W*aking up, Quinn opened her eyes then quickly closed them again and pulled the blanket over her head. The sun shining into her bedroom was almost blinding. Pulling the blanket away, she carefully opened her eyes once again, adjusting to the light as she did. Picking up her cell phone, she hit the button and tried to focus on the time.

My God, that was a rough night. I had far too much to drink and I sure as hell can't remember much past last call. I wonder how I got home...

Her question was answered when her thoughts were interrupted by a slight moan in the bed beside her and she quickly sat up.

Oh shit! Who are you?

She really didn't want to know but was sure she would find out soon enough from François who often teased 'that's what best friends are for'. Even so, he hated when she brought guys home with her. He always lectured how one-night stands were bad for her soul and for her heart. Deep down she knew he was right. Truth be told, she hated them too but committing to a relationship was difficult for her these days.

Getting out of bed, Quinn grabbed her torn grey track pants and faded blue sweatshirt and threw them on. François, an up and coming fashion designer, would cringe at the sight of them but she didn't care. They were her comfort clothes. Quickly peeking into her bedroom mirror, she cringed at the sight of herself. In recent months of unemployment she had managed to gain a few extra pounds and she wasn't pleased with the result, regardless of her still slim figure. Catching sight of the smudged mascara under her eyes, she frowned, and her auburn shoulder length hair was the worst case of bed head she had seen in quite awhile. Sighing, she grabbed a hair 'scrunchy' off her dresser and quickly pulled her hair back into a ponytail.

Looking over at her bed Quinn loudly said, "Hey!" When the stranger in her bed didn't move, she quickly became irritated. She wanted him gone.

"Hey! Sleeping beauty! Time to go home!" Her voice grew louder with each word she spoke, which didn't help given the pounding headache she was battling.

Again with the moaning.

Looking over at her latest hook-up she couldn't help but notice how good looking he was. Back in the day she would have considered a long-term commitment but not anymore. *That bastard, Spencer, ruined that for me when he decided to bed down every girl at the country club, which wouldn't have been an issue had we not only been in a committed relationship but also engaged at the time.*

'Forgive him' her parents had insisted; 'It's just the way things are nowadays' her sister assured her.

Why was I the only one in my family to actually have seen how blatantly wrong the whole scenario was, not to mention, humiliating.

She didn't care how rich Spencer was. The money wasn't worth the humiliation of him cheating on her and everyone at the country club knowing about it.

"Sleeping beauty! I said it's time for you to go. Now get out of my bed, get dressed and get the hell out!" She was irritable and didn't try to hide the fact.

"What?" The sleepy stranger was trying to get his bearings. "Why?" he asked groggily.

"Because I said so, that's why! Who said you could stay the night, anyway?"

It really was a rhetorical question because, although she couldn't remember, she knew it had been her. It was a standard weekend event for her these days, although she wasn't proud of it. She craved the affection but not the emotional commitment. She was lonely and she knew it but was afraid to commit after Spencer had broken her heart the year prior. It was almost as if moments like these were salve on an open wound that wouldn't heal.

"You did!" He was fully awake now and coming to the realization that Quinn wasn't going to be the love of his life, as promised the night before.

"We were supposed to go for breakfast this morning. You were going to introduce me to your parents."

Oh my God. You've got to be kidding.

Shaking her head in disbelief, Quinn offered, "Well, trust me, you don't want to meet my parents and they sure as hell don't want to meet you, so get out...now." Quinn walked out of the bedroom, down the hall and stood waiting by the kitchen. Her kitchen and living room were open concept offering a view straight down the hall towards her bedroom and to the right, a clear view of her front door.

Walking out half asleep and half dressed, Quinn had to admit that the stranger was quite handsome. Watching him walk towards her, she almost wished she hadn't decided to write off serious relationships.

"What is your problem?" he asked, confused by the turn of events. "Last night you were all about me staying and us getting to know each other better and today you're, 'get the hell out'."

Sighing with impatience, she said, "Oh well, I changed my mind. Too bad for you."

"Nice." The handsome stranger stood in front of her as he put his shirt on.

Quinn impatiently pointed. "The door is that way," she offered coldly.

"Wow, you are some cold bitch, you know that?" The handsome stranger headed towards the door, shoes in hand.

"Says you." She remained emotionless, not wanting to admit that his comment hurt deeply.

"Fuck you."

Hearing the door to her condominium slam behind him as he left, Quinn stood momentarily as tears came to her eyes but quickly shook them off and breathed a sigh of relief that she was once again alone. Heading to her bedroom she grabbed the sheets and blankets off her bed and threw them into the washing machine. Then she made her bed up with fresh sheets, opened her window slightly to let some of the cool early autumn air into her room while allowing the staleness of the night before, out.

Thinking of her parents, Quinn thought of the last conversation she had had with her mother the previous week and instantly grew angry. Nothing about her mother was warm and fuzzy and she and her parents sure as hell didn't have much of a relationship with each other. It also didn't help that as far as they were concerned, Quinn had walked away from the money and status her parents valued so much. Whenever she spoke with her mother, it was the same conversation over and over again.

"Why didn't you just stay with Spencer? He had money, charm, status, but no, not you, Quinn. You just refuse to be anything like your younger sister. Always having to rebel. You just could not settle for a proper life or, for that matter, just one man. For heaven's sake, Quinn, you might just as well put a red light outside your door with the number of men you bring home these days. This lifestyle of yours just isn't…" She hesitated, seemingly trying to gather her thoughts. "My God! Even that best friend of yours…"

"What? What about my best friend, Mother?"

"Well, you know."

"No, do tell." Quinn suspected what she was going to say.

"Well, he's queer. It's not normal."

"What's not normal, Mother? The fact that he's gay or the fact that he's actually my best friend?"

"Neither one of them is normal and the fact that you don't understand that, disturbs me." Her mother replied with distaste.

"Yet, you always go to his shop for clothing."

"Yes, of course. It's just business. F&F Fashions has a good reputation around the clubhouse and besides, those types of people are always good at fashion, now aren't they?"

The reply was so matter-of-fact and outside the realm of decency that Quinn had been momentarily speechless with disbelief.

"I just don't understand you, Quinn. You seem to think Spencer wasn't good enough and yet, here you are, living this reckless and, well, quite frankly, slutty lifestyle. It's disgraceful."

"And yet you had no issue with Spencer sleeping around with multiple women when we were engaged." Quinn coldly shot back.

"Spencer was just sowing his wild oats before he had to settle down with one woman. Nothing more. You would have done well to have understood that and just accepted it. You were completely unreasonable and you hurt him deeply when you left. It was humiliating for him, not to mention, for your father and I."

"Of course, it doesn't matter how I felt."

"Always the drama with you, Quinn. You always were overly sensitive about things that were of little importance."

"Thank you, Mother. You always did know how to make a girl feel good about herself."

Thinking back to that day, tears came to Quinn's eyes.

Truth be told, she hated the one-night stands. She longed for a relationship that would last, one that she could trust, one that had the warmth and desire of familiarity, comfort...true love. She just wasn't sure how to find it anymore or whether she even thought it was possible to find, for that matter.

"Somehow I don't think the universe has any plans for me to find true love." She talked to herself as she hopped in the shower. Feeling the hot water stream over her head and down her body, Quinn instantly relaxed. Washing away all remnants of the night before, she savoured the smell of the lavender shower gel and the floral-scented shampoo.

Getting out of the shower, she quickly dried off and threw on some clean jeans and a sweater. She felt so much better, as if the night before had never happened.

Hearing the phone ring, she ran to answer it. Seeing it was François she smiled and answered right away.

"François! What's up?"

"Wanna meet at Dills and Dolls for a latte? I'm in desperate need!"

"Absolutely! See you in about a half hour." Hanging up before François could respond, Quinn quickly dried her hair and threw it into a ponytail. Taking one last look at herself in the mirror she thought how her auburn hair was looking rather drab. *I could use some highlights but, oh well, what do I care? I'm not out to impress anyone these days.*

Grabbing her purse and jacket, she headed for the door but heard the phone ring. Running back to answer it she was pleased to hear her grandmother at the other end.

"Grandma! I'm so glad you called. How are you?"

"I'm fine, Quinn. How are you?"

"I'm doing great." Quinn smiled.

"When are you planning to come visit me, Dear?"

"Soon, I promise. I lost my job so I've been busy job hunting."

"Oh no! I'm sorry to hear that. Well, maybe it was for the best. Didn't you say your manager was a bit of a…how did you put it? Pervert?"

Laughing at her grandmother's directness, Quinn said, "Yup, he sure was." I actually slugged him the day I quit.

"What?! You slugged him? Why?"

"I was walking past him in the hall and he grabbed my ass. Instead of reporting it, I took matters into my own hands." Hearing her grandmother laugh made Quinn smile.

"When he threatened to have me charged, I told him to go ahead and I would be sure to let his wife know of his affair with the purchasing clerk, Blair."

"Oh my! I'm sure he wouldn't want his wife finding out about the other woman." Her grandmother offered.

"Man."

"Man? Blair is a man?"

"Yup."

Laughing, her grandmother offered, "You never were one to put up with nonsense, Quinn. I'm proud of you."

Her grandmother's praise wasn't necessary but certainly welcome. They had a very close relationship and she couldn't think of anyone she admired more. Her grandmother wasn't your stereotypical grandmother. She was more forward thinking, open-minded and so much younger than the eighty-five years her birth certificate indicated.

"Grandma, can I call you later? I'm just on my way out the door to meet up with François."

"Of course, my Dear. I'll be home. Say hello to him for me, won't you? He's such a lovely young man."

Like night and day, my mother and grandmother. Hard to believe one was raised by the other.

Minutes later, walking through her condo lobby, Quinn saw the concierge speaking with her elderly neighbour.

"Hey, George!" Quinn waved as she walked past his desk.

"Good morning, Miss Fairchild. Nice to see you this fine Autumn day." George waved and went back to speaking to the confused woman in front of his desk.

"...I'm telling you, George, I don't understand why the taxi hasn't shown up. You called him over an hour ago."

"Mrs. Martin, you never asked me to call you a taxi, however, I would be most happy to call one for you now."

And with that, Quinn was through the door and out onto one of the busiest streets of the downtown theatre district. It wasn't even noon yet and the hustle and bustle of the street was already in full-swing. It was one of the things Quinn loved about her neighbourhood. It was full of life. Lots of theatres, cafés, nightclubs and restaurants that she was convinced represented every country in the world with the diversity of foods offered.

TWO

rriving at Dills and Dolls, her favourite coffee shop, Quinn saw François waving from their usual table at the back of the shop but she first headed to the counter to order a latte. They both loved the name of the place. Though peoples' dirty imaginations ran amok, the place was, in fact, named after Dolly Cranberg, who owned the place and who loved dill pickles. It was small and cozy, yet modern, and their 'go to' spot ever since it opened several years prior. Being at Dills and Dolls with her friend was Quinn's happy place.

Grabbing her drink and heading to the back of the café, Quinn was stopped by Sasha.

"Quinn! Are you coming to yoga tonight? We haven't seen you in weeks."

This was an unwelcome interruption in her day. Sasha was the owner of the Hotness Yoga and Spa. When Quinn lost her job, François had recommended yoga to her. She idiotically went to one class, hoping to shut François up about it. As anticipated, she hated it and never went back. Now, every time Sasha sees Quinn she stops her to ask when she will be coming back to yoga again.

Sasha is so annoyingly happy. She always has that 'glass is half full', positive attitude that I despise so much. She's just too...what's the word for it...right...nice! She's too fucking nice!

Sighing out loud, Quinn didn't stop walking as she said, "Sasha, I told you the last time you asked me, yoga isn't my thing." Continuing to walk towards the back of the café, Quinn could hear Sasha's standard response,

"Yes, but Quinn, I think if you gave it another try you would grow to like it." Watching Quinn walking away from her, Sasha added, "Well, we are always here if you change your mind. It was great to see you again, Quinn! Namaste!"

Oh, for Chrissakes!

Sitting down across from François, she said, "I fucking hate you!"

"I see Sasha caught you again." He laughed.

"Does that woman ever stop smiling? I've never met anyone so bloody nice in my life." Quinn rolled her eyes.

"Gee, thanks!" François laughed.

"And why is everyone so into yoga these days anyway? I find it completely irritating. I can't sit still that long. I hate the breathing in and out, in and out. The whole thing is just a fucking fad!"

Laughing, François added, "Yeah, a fad that has lasted thousands of years."

"Whatever." Quinn grumbled.

François Bonnaire had been Quinn's best friend for many years since they first met at a small theatrical production a mutual friend was in. Quinn remembered being very captivated by François, as most women were with him. During intermission, they met at the venue bar and instantly bonded when they expressed how much they hated the play and regrettably, how terrible their friend was at acting. They had been best friends ever since.

Looking across the table at him now, she never put a lot of thought to it but she understood why women found him so attractive. It was because he was. *He's tall, very handsome with that deep voice and those intense dark brown eyes...*

Studying her friend for a moment she thought, *His brunette hair has that tousled sexy look to it, then combine it with that innate charm of his...well, admittedly, it's the icing on the cake if you ask me...until, that is, those women find themselves heartbroken to learn he's gay.* Quinn chuckled at the thought. She had seen it happen many times since meeting François. She almost pitied those women as they walked away disappointed.

Shaking her thoughts away, she smiled. Other than her grandmother, there was no one she would rather spend time with.

"So, did you still want me to come to Sarah's wedding with you next weekend or have you finally found a date to replace me?" François was sure of the answer to his question.

"No date, and yes, I want you to come with me."

"Oh thank God! I love weddings. Nothing makes me happier than to attend a wedding with you." The sarcasm didn't go unnoticed.

"The speeches, the tears, the poorly dressed…I mean, I just can't get enough." Laughing, François took a sip of his latte. "Maybe one day you will actually have a significant other that you could take instead of me," he teased.

"Yeah, yeah." Quinn rolled her eyes.

"So, what time did you leave the club last night? Did you grab a taxi with the others?"

"Well, not exactly…" Quinn bit down on her bottom lip.

"What does that mean?" François was confused.

"Well, I didn't grab a cab with the others."

"Okay, well how did you get home?" Not getting a response, François suddenly realized what happened.

"You didn't go home with that guy…"

Cringing, Quinn cautiously looked at her friend.

"Oh my God, Quinn! You need to stop doing that. It will destroy you emotionally. You know I hate it when you take guys home. It's not safe."

"Yeah, I know, I know." Quinn was remorseful.

"Do I really need to be going over this again with you?" François wasn't angry, just very annoyed with his friend.

"No." She responded sheepishly.

Sighing heavily, François asked, "So, what time do we have to leave?"

"For what?" Quinn was confused.

"The wedding!"

"Oh, right. Well, it's an afternoon wedding and since I'm a bridesmaid, I need to be there early afternoon for pictures, so I hope you can find yourself something to do. I'm sure there will be a bar you can spend time at though."

"I'm sure." François replied still somewhat annoyed with her. "Except I can't drink because I'm the designated driver, remember?"

"Ah, right, I forgot." Quinn hadn't forgotten and François knew it. Changing the subject Quinn lamented, "I can't believe I actually agreed to be a bloody bridesmaid. If Sarah wasn't such a good friend…anyway, I hate the thought of having to wear a strapless, skin-tight dress and heels for chrissakes. You know how much I hate dressing up and don't get me started about having to wear make-up." Quinn knew she was whining but couldn't help herself.

"It will do you good to dress up for a change. You're a beautiful woman, Q, and you waste it away wearing those God-awful clothes you own and you haven't done a thing with your hair in God knows how long." Thinking for a moment, he asked, "How long *has* it been?" He stopped to ponder his own question. "Anyway, it's time to get a good cut and colour, girl. Even some highlights would do you wonders."

"You're not at work, François and I'm not one of your models." Quinn mused.

"Oh, don't I know it," he laughed. "All I can say is thank God for this wedding. I can't wait to see how you turn out after you get your hair and make-up done at Maurice's. I likely won't recognize you. *You* likely won't recognize you!"

Quinn shook her head and laughed. "If you weren't a fashion designer, I don't think you would be quite so critical of my looks, do you?"

Giving her the 'once over', François said, "Oh, I wouldn't say that…"

THREE

*S*arah's wedding arrived faster than Quinn had wanted but they were friends from university and Quinn would never have let her friend down no matter how much she hated dressing up. She was just happy Sarah found Sam and ditched Travis. *That guy was such an asshole,* Quinn thought. *Travis and Spencer are like two cheating peas in a pod.*

Quinn opted to go to a hair salon in the city rather than meet up with the other ladies at the salon closer to the wedding. François recommended Maurice's Salon and Spa and she trusted his judgement. Besides, he was paying.

Quinn had arrived bright and early and although it was a long morning she had to admit that the several painstaking hours were worth it.

The highlights the stylist put in her hair and the cut he gave her made her look years younger. Next came the make-up.

They better not make me look like a fucking clown, otherwise it will come right back off again, she thought as she prepared for the worst.

As it turned out, she worried for nothing. They did a fantastic job of her make-up. It almost didn't look like she had any make-up on at all yet she looked so much prettier, if she did say so herself.

Once she was ready to leave, Quinn peered into the mirror one last time. She had opted to let her hair fall freely to her shoulders and she had to admit she loved how the curls bounced gently as she moved. Looking at herself, Quinn smiled. She actually looked, and more importantly, felt, pretty. A feeling that had eluded her for a very long time.

Heading home again, Quinn put on the bridesmaid dress, lamenting about the fact that it was still too loose at the top. She must have told the dressmaker at least three times to adjust it tighter and all three times Quinn was told there was nothing wrong with the fit. She finally gave up trying.

Thank God I'm only going to be wearing the damn dress once.

François arrived right on time to pick Quinn up. Waiting for her, he got out of the car and walked around ready to open the passenger car door. Hearing her speaking to the concierge, François looked up in time to see her come outside and instantly became speechless as he watched her walk towards him. He was actually dumbstruck. He had never seen his friend look more beautiful in all the years he had known her. She looked absolutely gorgeous today.

Seeing the look on his face, Quinn immediately grew defensive. "What!?"

"Oh, nothing." He opened the door and motioned for her to get into the car. "Except, I've never seen you look more beautiful."

Getting into the car, Quinn said, "Don't make fun of me, François. You know how self-conscious I get with you about how I dress especially whenever I dress up, as rare as that can be."

"I'm not kidding, Q. My God, you look stunning!"

Quinn waited for François to get back into the car and smiled at the compliment. She felt good and it was nice to hear that she looked it too.

Starting the car up, François said, "Now, let's go wow those bitches!"

FOUR

The wedding was just outside of the city at a lake resort near where Sarah's parents lived. Pulling up in front of the place, Quinn was in awe of what a spectacular venue it was.

The day went by quickly and as far as weddings went. It had been a perfect sunny fall day of wedded bliss for her friend. Quinn had to admit that Sarah's had been one of the most beautiful weddings she had ever been a part of and that her friend was one of the most beautiful brides she had ever seen. Quinn had often dreamed of something similar but gave up on that dream when she left Spencer more than a year ago.

Quinn had been very proud to stand up as a bridesmaid for Sarah along with Sarah's sister, Terri, and her maid of honour, Chloe. Quinn was especially thrilled that Sarah had finally found a great guy like Sam who made her happy and treated her so well. They had only been together for just over a year but Sarah and Sam seemed like they were the perfect match.

After dinner, Quinn needed some fresh air and decided to go for a walk. It was dusk and walking down to the dock, she sat in one of the Adirondack chairs. She admired the magnificent sunset seemingly melting into the earth. Infatuated with the glowing golds and warm oranges, she likened the sight to the embers of a fire that had long been burning and would soon extinguish. She was enjoying the beauty and tranquility of this moment.

Putting on the sweater she had brought with her, Quinn closed her eyes in silent meditation, enjoying the gentle breeze that seemed to have picked up. Thinking for a moment, she would never have fessed up to François, that, although she hated all the fussing-up, she had to admit she felt pretty damn hot.

"You know, you're missing a great party back up the hill."

Quinn was taken by surprise to discover she was no longer alone. Looking up she wasn't in the least bit disappointed to see an extremely good-looking man walking onto the dock. *Talk about tall, dark and handsome,* she thought admiringly.

"I suppose you're right, but it's quiet out here on the dock…and I have to admit I'm rather enjoying the good looking view." Realizing what she had mistakenly implied, Quinn became somewhat uncharacteristically flustered. "What I mean is, the view is quite captivating." Rolling her eyes she tried one last time to save herself.

Sighing she offered. "It's just nice to have a few minutes of quiet time." *What the hell? Since when do I get all flustered because of some guy?*

The handsome stranger chuckled as he listened to her flounder and took his place standing at the end of the dock, quietly enjoying the view over the water. A few moments later he turned to look at her and responded, "You're right. The view is quite captivating."

Feeling herself blushing, Quinn looked down and fidgeted, wiping imaginary dust off her dress.

Damn! What's wrong with me? Since when do I stammer over my words? Why can't I just say something without embarrassing myself?

"I'm Darcy, friend of the groom."

"Quinn Fairchild, friend of the bride." Smiling Quinn began to relax after her embarrassing moment.

"Feel free to join me if you like. There is clearly no shortage of chairs." She laughed as she indicated the half dozen or more empty chairs sitting on the dock and along the shoreline.

Darcy sat down beside Quinn and pulled a couple of beers out of his pockets and offered her one, which she gladly accepted.

"You came prepared." Quinn popped off the cap and took a welcome sip of the cold beer.

"That I did. It's about the only way to get through yet another wedding."

Quinn couldn't help but quietly concur.

"So, Quinn, why are you sitting here all by yourself? Where's your date? Passed out drunk somewhere? Flirting with another woman? Or are you single and sitting here waiting for a nice guy like me to sweep you off your feet?"

Boy, this guy gets straight to the point doesn't he? Glancing over at him she quickly looked away again. *Although, he does seem rather charming and he really is quite good looking.*

"Well, I'm certainly not sitting here waiting to be swept off my feet and if you must know, my date, François, is a friend of mine. He's definitely not passed out anywhere because he's the designated driver tonight, and well, as much as he himself is a big flirt, you will most likely find the women flirting with him. They can never seem to help themselves because he's so charming and a ton of fun, however, the most likely scenario is that you'll find him flirting with one of the groomsmen because François is gay." Quinn laughed.

Quinn always had fun with François and whenever she needed a date for a function she would ask him because the party always got started when he arrived and Quinn loved him for that. Quinn had also been François' 'date' on several occasions and she reluctantly had to admit that he was likely a lot more fun as a date than she was.

Smiling as he listened, when Quinn finished speaking, Darcy didn't say anything at first then finally offered,

"Okay, well, if you must know…"

Huh?

"…I actually have a blind date, who does drink, and is actually passed out at our table in the corner after having flirted with some guy sitting beside her throughout dinner. Although she is not my lesbian friend filling in as my date, I can assure you that I am single and available for the taking..."

The entire time he spoke he never even looked at Quinn until he finished and then looking her way, he added with a sheepish grin, "...as I'm positive, that, at this very moment you're thinking what a great catch I would make."

Oh my God! Laughing, Quinn thought, *This guy is a little full of himself but I have to give it to him, he has a very charming mannerism, and smile, and he certainly doesn't lack confidence. In fact, he seems to have plenty to spare.*

"So I take it your date hasn't paid much attention to you all night long which I gather you aren't used to." Quinn couldn't help the slight sarcasm. Habit.

"Oh trust me, I'm used to it." Darcy took another swig of beer and stared out over the water.

Did I catch a hint of emotion? Quinn wondered, almost feeling sorry for the guy. Saying nothing, she took another drink of her beer, enjoying the rather unexpected moment that had developed.

"So what's your story, Quinn? Why no boyfriend?"

Hmmm, this guy isn't shy at all and who says I need a boyfriend anyway?

Her defences began going up bit by bit. Quinn didn't like talking about her past and wasn't about to start now. Thinking carefully, she wasn't sure how to respond so didn't answer at all.

"So, what you're saying, or rather, not saying, is that you're available and looking." Darcy summarized.

Wow! I wonder if he always vocalizes what he thinks?

"No, I'm not saying that at all and can assure you I am not looking, whatsoever." She couldn't explain it but this guy annoyed, yet intrigued her at the same time. "And do you always ask inappropriate questions of people you've just met?" she quizzed.

Looking at her, Darcy seemed puzzled. "What's inappropriate about what I asked? I figure that there is no point in beating around the bush. I hate games, believe me, I've had enough played on me in the past to last a lifetime. Wouldn't you rather date someone who's straight forward with nothing to hide rather than someone like your ex who clearly cheated on you and left you wondering how you never saw it coming?"

Quickly looking up at Darcy, Quinn abruptly responded, "Who says he cheated…?" Catching herself, Quinn stopped talking. Although he was correct, she was indignant that he would make such an assumption. *Honestly, this guy is unbelievable.*

"Well didn't he?"

Quinn hesitated to answer but reluctantly offered, "I don't like to discuss my previous relationships."

Nodding, he continued, "So, he cheated on you and then when you called him up on it he said he would never do it again if you would just stay with him, that it had only happened once, that it was only sex and it meant nothing…"

Stopping, Darcy looked at Quinn who was staring out at the sunset that had almost completely disappeared.

"…that it was you he truly loved." Darcy couldn't take his eyes off Quinn, looking for any reaction, whatsoever.

After a few moments, Darcy cleared his throat and continued, "Hey, listen, don't worry about it. The same thing happened to me once. You'd think I would have learned by now but I have kept trying in the hopes that I would finally find the right girl."

"And do you honestly think you will find the right girl?" She asked skeptically.

Softening, he looked knowingly at Quinn then turned away and said, "Oh, I've found the right girl, alright."

"How can you be so sure?"

"I just knew it the moment I met her." Hesitating, he added, "She just hasn't realized it yet."

"Well, aren't you just the romantic?" Realizing how cynical she sounded Quinn offered, "Hey listen, I'm sorry, that was uncalled for."

"Don't worry about it – I don't get offended easily."

"Well, I thought I met the right guy…once. But he wasn't the right guy for me, so much as he was right for my parents. I have my doubts I'll ever find the right guy." She sounded pessimistic because she was. She also wondered why she felt compelled to pour her feelings out to this stranger.

The two sat in quiet contemplation.

"So what about you?" Quinn asked, more to change the subject than out of actual interest. "Why don't you have a girlfriend? You're a good looking guy."

"Oh, you think so, do you?" Darcy grinned at Quinn who immediately blushed.

"You know what I mean," she said.

Darcy sat for a moment before answering. "Well, my story is a little different. I was married for two years when my wife announced that she had been seeing someone and was leaving me for them."

"I'm sorry to hear that." Quinn was sincere.

"Well, as it turned out, she was in love with someone whose name was Sylvia."

"Oh, I see." Quinn said quietly. "That must have been difficult."

"It was, but we remain good friends. They married a few years ago and moved to California. There are no hard feelings."

"And you've never met anyone else?" Quinn couldn't help but pry. He had caught her interest.

"I've dated on and off." Darcy took one last chug of his beer and placed the empty under his chair. Pulling out another beer he asked, "You want another?"

"Sure, why not?" Quinn drank back the last of her first one and placed the bottle under her chair and accepted the other from Darcy. "How many pockets did you stash beer into?" she laughed.

Opening their beers, Darcy and Quinn tapped bottles together in a silent toast to each other then sat for a few moments quietly enjoying the beauty of the stars now shining in the sky and the moon glowing undisturbed across the calm lake.

The time went by quickly as they talked and laughed until Quinn began to feel chilled from the cool night air. She couldn't remember the last time she felt so comfortable or had enjoyed herself so much with a guy and was surprisingly reluctant for it to end but it was getting late and she knew she should get back to the reception.

"Well, I suppose I had better go in, I'm starting to get cold. These bridesmaid dresses aren't exactly made for warmth...or comfort, for that matter, and this sweater isn't exactly warm either." Quinn stood up. "It really has been nice meeting you, Darcy, but I suppose I should go save François from all the swooning women. Honestly, they love him. I personally think François feeds off all the attention though." Laughing, Quinn picked up the empty beer bottles from underneath her chair.

Darcy stood up and grabbed his empties. "I'll walk up with you. I need a refill."

FIVE

When they arrived back from the dock most guests were managing to work their way onto the dance floor. Quinn smiled and stood affectionately watching François charm Sarah's mother and grandmother. It was very clear they were smitten with him.

I love François so much. He adds such life to every party he's at. Quinn laughed out loud as she saw her charming friend grab Sarah's grandmother by the hand and coax her onto the dance floor with him. Grandma Gladys was smiling from ear to ear and not surprisingly, François managed to get her dancing to the Rolling Stones song, "Satisfaction", of all things. Quinn shook her head in amazement.

I must say Grandma Gladys is actually a pretty good dancer. Laughing, Quinn thought, *François seems to be able to get anyone dancing with just his enthusiasm alone.* Smiling as she watched him, she thought, *I wish I could be more like him.*

Remembering Darcy, Quinn looked around to see if he was anywhere to be found. She hadn't seen him since they walked back from the dock together. After a few minutes she questioned why she even cared, gave up looking and focused her attention on François and his next exploit. Apparently, Sarah's maid-of-honour, Chloe, was the big winner and was at this very moment being spun around on the dance floor with great expertise. *Those ladies won't know what hit them,* Quinn laughed. Yet again, François was the life of the party.

Before she knew it, the bride and groom had finished their last dance and the D.J. was hailing last call for the bar and announcing the final song of the night. Walking over to the bar Quinn had just picked up a drink when she suddenly felt someone's arm go around her waist and she jumped from the unexpected surprise.

"Hey, pretty lady, want to dance?"

It was Darcy. Quinn had to admit that she was mildly intrigued by his magnetism.

"I'm not much for dancing." She tried to evade him.

"Well, no point going home tonight disappointed that you didn't dance with me so I'm not taking no for an answer." Darcy took the drink out of her hand and placed it back down on the bar.

Laughing, she reluctantly agreed and he spun her out onto the dance floor where they danced the final slow dance of the night. She assumed he had to be at least six feet tall since her head just reached his shoulder. He was a good dancer and she had to concede she was enjoying the moment with him. He made her smile, which was hard to do these days.

"So how about going out with me on Friday night, Quinn? I would love to get to know you better."

Quinn couldn't explain why she felt intrigued at the prospect but was reluctant to follow through.

"No. I don't think so."

"Oh c'mon. I may not be as painfully good looking as Sam but I am a great guy. Go out with me and if you don't have a good time then we can discuss a second date."

"What do you mean? Even if I did have a good time with you, what makes you think I would even consider a second date with you at all? You're a little too bold for my taste." Quinn couldn't believe how self-confident he was.

"I'm not going to stop asking until you say yes." Leaning in, Darcy whispered into her ear, "I'm a really great kisser and I make a mean lasagna. You can't lose."

Quinn smiled and ever so slightly melted. Closing her eyes, she had to admit that his charm was hard to ignore especially given the ambiance of the room with the smooth, romantic sound of the music and the soft glow of the lights.

"You don't even know me. I'm not the person you think I am."

Taking a deep breath in, Quinn was quite captivated by the subtle aroma of Darcy's cologne and found herself becoming lost in the moment.

"Really? Well, the person I think you are is beautiful, straight-forward and someone I want to see again." Darcy wasn't at all hesitant when he spoke. "It's not complicated."

Opening her eyes again, she offered, "I don't think you would particularly like me."

"Oh, I dunno. Why don't you let me be the judge of that." Darcy smiled. "I'm a big boy, I can handle myself. You don't seem so scary to me."

Sighing, Quinn wasn't sure what direction to take with this guy. *He's persistent, I'll give him that.*

"Well, we may live hundreds of miles apart. What makes you think that it's even feasible?" Quinn was unexpectedly disappointed at the possibility although she would never have admitted it. He was the first guy since Spencer who she genuinely found herself interested in and it was disconcerting.

"I asked Sam. I know exactly where you live, about twenty minutes across town from me. So what do you say? Will you go out with me?"

Quinn was amazed that Darcy had gone so far as to ask Sam but strangely felt elated at the thought. She hadn't been this excited at the possibility of a date in a very long time but she was still very guarded. It took her a moment before she responded.

"Okay fine. I'll go out with you, on one date and if I don't have a good time well that's it. You hit the road. No second date." She was determined to sound firm on the matter and the reality was, that second dates were never an option for her these days anyway.

"Well, okay, Quinn, but I can assure you that after one date with me you'll be wanting to go on a second." Darcy twirled her around to the music, then pulling her in, held her unnervingly close.

"Well…we'll see…," Quinn suddenly had trouble speaking. She was flustered being held so close to Darcy. Closing her eyes once again, she took a moment to catch her breath. She was far more captivated than she was comfortable admitting.

Damn his cologne smells good.

Regaining her composure, Quinn tried to pull away from Darcy but he wasn't having anything to do with that and held her tight.

Oh boy. This is actually…quite…nice.

Oh no I don't! Quinn tried once again to regain her composure. *What the heck is wrong with me? Get it together girl!* This was proving more difficult than expected.

The song ended and the lights came up. Quickly pulling away from Darcy, Quinn cleared her throat and tried unsuccessfully to will herself to speak. She couldn't look him in the eyes but instead looked down and straightened her dress out.

"I'll call you this week to set things up for Friday. Sarah gave me your number saying something to the effect of, it's about time you dated a great guy like me." Shrugging, he added, "What can I say…" then knowingly grinned at Quinn whose heart ever so slightly fluttered.

"Um…well…I'm thinking maybe it isn't such a good idea after all…" Biting down on her bottom lip Quinn wasn't comfortable and needed to leave. "I've got to go." Turning to leave, Quinn felt Darcy gently grab her arm.

"Don't run out on me now, Quinn. Just go out with me Friday. I assure you, you won't regret it. I won't take no for an answer." Darcy smiled, then, without warning, pulled Quinn into his arms, passionately kissed her then left quickly before she had a chance to gather her wits about her.

Once she was able to catch her breath, Quinn opened her eyes in time to see Darcy walking away. Stunned by what had just taken place she was having difficulty thinking straight.

"Wow," she whispered to herself as she ran a hand through her hair.

Shaking herself back to reality, Quinn looked around to see if anyone had noticed, relieved they hadn't.

"Yeah, I don't think so and why would Sarah give him my number?" Quinn's uncertainty was rearing its ugly head and her flight response was kicking in rapidly. *I have no intention of putting myself in a position of heartbreak again for you or anyone else, Darcy, whoever you are.*

She needed to go and she needed to go right now. Looking around for François and her ride home, she finally caught sight of him across the room kissing the top of Sarah's grandmother's hand. Quinn rolled her eyes, smiling at his undeniable charm with the ladies.

Seeing her approach him, Quinn could hear François say to Grandma Gladys, "Well m'lady, I must be off. I must take Cinderella home. She's not exactly the patient type." He laughed as he embellished and with a bow to Sarah's grandmother, François caught up to Quinn and delighted in teasing her.

Standing with his hand on one hip, François conjured up the most feminine voice he could and asked, "Hey girlfriend, who's that gorgeous hunk of man you were dancing with? I haven't seen him around and I must admit I was a wee bit jealous."

"Stop, François. You know how I hate when you talk like that. Why do you do that to me?" Quinn frowned.

Laughing, François reverted back to his own voice which was, in fact, quite deep and sexy sounding. She often said he sounded like your stereotypical radio disc jockey.

"Aw c'mon, Q, you know I'm just having some fun with you but seriously he's one good looking hunk of man. Where did you find him?"

She smiled when François called her Q. She loved the nickname her friend had given her when they first met. He said it made him think of the James Bond character and as she came to realize, François absolutely loved James Bond movies. He was the only one who called her that and she loved that sense of familiarity their friendship had. Grabbing her handbag, Quinn updated François on the events of the evening with Darcy as they left the hall for his car.

"…and, if you can believe it, he asked me out on Friday night." she concluded as they began to drive away.

"You are going, aren't you?" François asked knowing how his friend could be.

"No, of course not! Why would I? I don't even know the guy." Quinn waited for the rebuttal she was sure to get.

"Well, if he's a friend of Sam's, I would think he's likely a decent guy. Maybe someone you could get to know better than a one-night stand. Someone not like Spencer…"

"This has nothing to do with Spencer! I'm just not interested in a serious relationship. Didn't work for me before and it won't work for me now." Quinn was annoyed with her friend.

"Oh, I get it."

"You get what?!" She asked defensively.

"Just that, if you aren't the one with the upper hand, you're too afraid to follow through." François offered. "He went after you so…"

"That's not true!" Quinn interrupted.

"Oh, but it is true, Q. You're a big 'ole chicken and just won't admit it! I think you're afraid to go out with him in case he's someone who could actually deal with your bullshit."

"Oh my God, François, you're grasping at straws. I'm not afraid to go out with him. I'm not afraid of any man, you know that." Deep down Quinn knew this statement wasn't entirely true and had a hard time trying to sound convincing, even for herself.

"Well, usually, I would say that's true but now that I see how you are reacting about this guy, I'm not so sure." François goaded his friend.

"Why are you being such a jerk, François?"

Sitting quietly, Quinn wasn't sure how to respond. *That little French bastard makes me so mad!* François' comments angered her more because she knew he was right.

"Okay, fine! I'll go out with him on Friday night and that's it. No second date just like the others. That should shut your big French mouth up once and for all."

"Nope. If he asks you out on a second date you have to go. That's the deal. If you still aren't interested then I will concede but you have to give it at least two dates with this guy…oh, and no overnights. You need to give it your best shot." Thinking for a moment, François added, "And I expect you to put nice clothes on, do your hair, maybe even a little bit of make-up…put some effort into it."

"You have some nerve, you know that? You can't tell me what I can and can't do. You have no say in this matter other than I will commit to two dates only." Quinn was defiant. "And don't worry about me sleeping with him, I'm not interested anyway." She lied like she had never lied before.

"Oh, I have plenty to say in the matter and I'm telling you that those are the rules! If I have to come over there and dress you myself, I will!" He was purposely standing his ground. Something about Darcy made his friend uncomfortable. She didn't realize it but he saw how she reacted when Darcy kissed her. That man had her hook, line and sinker and he wasn't about to let Quinn walk away from this one.

"But…"

"No 'but's', Q. You need to get happy again." François was determined not to back down.

"I am happy…" Quinn retorted.

"The hell you are! So, like it or not, you're going on those two dates and putting your best foot forward…and that's final!"

Pulling onto the highway for home, François added, "And anyway, you need someone else as your date besides me for a change. It gets exhausting always being the life of the party," he teased his friend.

SIX

*I*t had been five days since the wedding and Quinn hadn't said one word about Darcy to François. Arriving at Dills and Dolls, François looked for Quinn and seeing her, waved hello and headed to the counter to order his usual latte. François knew it was typical of his friend to avoid anything she didn't want to be questioned on. What *she* didn't realize was that he wasn't about to allow her that luxury this time around.

Grabbing his drink, François walked over and sat down across from Quinn and didn't waste any time before asking, "Sooo, are you excited about your date tomorrow with Darcy?"

"No! Of course I'm not!" Quinn was overly indignant and knew it. Sighing, she took a sip of her chai tea latte.

François could only shake his head, not at all surprised by the answer. *Typical Quinn.*

"But I'm going to go."

François raised his eyebrows. "Oh, really?! Okay...good...I think." *I really didn't expect that. I thought for sure she would back out of our deal.*

"Why?" Prodding her, he wanted to be sure it wasn't a trap. He didn't trust her when she became agreeable. "I mean, it's great that you are, but why aren't you fighting me on this?"

"Now, don't start with me, François. Let's be perfectly clear. I'm not going because you told me I have to...well, okay...I am a little, but let me remind you that I am not in the least bit interested in this guy and

I know what you are going to say. I need to get out there. It's time to start living life again. I need someone in my life besides you. I need more than one-night stands. Well, I'm telling you right now that I don't care about any of that, I'm only going on this date to be polite because he's Sam's friend and I don't have the heart to break our date. I just won't go out on a second with him, that's all. I mean, after all, I'm fine on my own. I'm a strong, independent woman. I certainly don't need to be in a 'relationship'…" This was said with great animosity. "My God! He's far too confident and outspoken for me. I mean, the guy asked me about my past relationships! Right out of the blue! It's none of his damn business! He doesn't even know me! Can you believe he actually assumes I'll go on a second date with him? I mean seriously, he's delusional…"

Quinn was nervously ranting and briefly looked up in time to see François staring in the direction of the door, seemingly not listening to her.

"Why aren't you listening to me?" Looking in the same direction she couldn't understand what was drawing his attention. "François! You haven't heard a word I've said!"

"Sasha just came in. Does that woman ever wear anything besides those damn yoga pants? I mean really…" François was frowning as he spoke.

"What!?" Quinn couldn't believe what she was hearing.

"Look at them! They're hideous!"

Quinn looked over at Sasha then back at François. "Are you kidding me?"

"No, I'm not! They're dreadful!"

"François!"

"What?!" Looking back at Quinn, he seemed oblivious to how annoyed she had become.

"You aren't even listening to me!"

"Yes, I am listening to you." François responded.

"No, you aren't! You didn't hear a word I said." Quinn was frustrated. She waited impatiently for her friend to respond.

François had a blank look on his face as he said, matter-of-factly, "So you like him, then."

"You're an ass, you know that?" Quinn took another sip of her latte, annoyed with her friend but unwilling to leave because Sasha was sitting by the door and she was the last person Quinn wanted to deal with right now.

Just then Quinn's phone rang and seeing that it was her grandmother she quickly answered it.

"Hi Grandma! How are you doing?"

"Yes, the wedding went very well. Sarah looked absolutely stunning!"

"Yes, of course I'm planning on visiting, very soon. I can't wait! How are things at the cabin?"

"That's great!"

Quinn rolled her eyes as she watched François get up and walk over to Sasha's table. She watched as he sat down and started speaking with Sasha very animatedly, pointing to her yoga pants as he did so.

"Oh, they are the same as usual. You know what mother is like. I swear we can't have a conversation without having an argument."

"They drive me crazy too and, no, I don't pay any attention to what they say, I promise." She had to lie about this. She didn't want to worry her grandmother.

"No, I haven't found a job yet and I don't need any money, I'm fine. Thank you."

"No, I have no intention of ever borrowing from my parents, I can assure you."

"Yes, I promise. If I need money I will call you, don't worry."

"Yes, as a matter-of-fact, I'm with him right now."

"I will, and François sends you his love, too. I'll call you next week. Love you. Bye!"

Hanging up, Quinn couldn't help but chuckle at the sight of François talking with Sasha. *He has more nerve than the two of us put together.*

Watching as he stood back up to leave, Quinn shook her head when she saw him hand a business card over to Sasha then walk over to grab another latte.

Returning to their table, François sat down once again with Quinn.

"So, that was your Grandmama."

"Yes, and she sends you her love. So, what were you talking to Sasha about?" Not that she really needed to ask.

"I told you, those yoga pants are hideous…" François glanced back towards Sasha.

"You have some nerve…"

"What?! Someone needed to tell her." François watched as Sasha got up from her table, looked in his direction, smiled and waved good-bye before leaving the café.

"And you felt that someone should be you." Knowing her friend the way she did, Quinn wasn't particularly surprised François had the nerve to confront Sasha about her yoga pants.

"Well, of course! Who better to tell her than me?" François seemed shocked by her comment. Looking back at Quinn, François asked, "So, how is dear ole granny?"

"She's good." Quinn answered before taking another sip of her latte.

"I still can't see how your mother and grandmother could be mother and daughter. They are nothing alike. Your grandmother is the most unpretentious person I've ever met and believe me, I know *many* pretentious people, including myself!" François was quite serious.

"Trust me, if it wasn't for the fact that they were related, I'm sure my mother wouldn't even bother with her. My grandmother always said that my father ruined her. Once mother met him, she became enthralled with money and status and as you know, my grandparents were never about that."

"Well, your grandmother is such a sweetheart." François sincerely meant what he said. "I must admit that I'm amazed your grandmother still lives in that cabin though. I thought your parents wanted her to move closer to them after your grandfather died."

"Oh my God! She would never live close to my parents. No, she's very happy at the cabin and she has no reason to leave. Her health is good and she hires people to do the work around there and besides, I wouldn't want her to leave. I love going there. It's so peaceful and relaxing. I can't imagine her selling it. I spent all my growing up years going there for summer vacations and holidays. My parents always complained about going. So did my sister, for that matter, but I loved it. Still do."

"Well, I know I couldn't live there. It's too remote for me. I need the hustle and bustle of the city." François was a city-boy through and through.

"One day I'll get you there for a visit."

"Don't count on it. If I don't hear sirens and horns honking every few minutes I would lose my mind." Thinking for a moment, François asked, "By the way, does your grandmother know you have a big date on Friday night?"

"No! There is no need to tell her. It won't amount to anything anyway."

"So *you* say…" François teased.

SEVEN

*F*riday arrived and Quinn was strangely nervous about meeting up with Darcy. She hated to admit that she really was attracted to him…it made her uncomfortable. She generally didn't feel this way about dating anyone and it was making her uneasy. *I'm so glad I said I would meet him at the pub. That way I can make an excuse to leave sooner rather than later.*

Walking into the Beagle at Bay pub, Quinn looked around for Darcy. She knew she was a few minutes early. Looking around she was relieved that he had yet to arrive and decided to get a booth.

Grabbing a beer from the bar and sitting down, Quinn directed her attention to the band that was playing. *These guys are pretty good.* Enjoying her few minutes of alone time before Darcy arrived, Quinn noticed an older, beer-bellied man walking towards her from the bar. He had a brush-cut, scruffy beard and was wearing a stained white t-shirt, baggy jeans that sat under his belly and he looked to be staggering.

"Hey there, pretty lady, you look lonely. How's about I sit here and keep ya company?"

He was slurring his words and swayed as he tried to stand in one place. He was clearly drunk and Quinn had no intention of allowing him to join her. Without turning her head, Quinn looked up at him with only her eyes and said, "Thanks but my friend will be here any minute. You have a nice night though." Trying her best to discourage him, Quinn soon realized he wasn't so easily dissuaded.

"Well that's okay, pretty lady, I don't mind waiting with you until your friend gets here." Finishing his sentence the man hiccupped then belched loudly. Quinn could smell the alcohol on his breath and turned her head away to avoid the worst of it.

"Oh that was a good one." The drunken stranger offered as he sat down in the booth across from her. Quinn looked around to see if anyone was paying attention and of course they were all too focused on the band to bother noticing her dilemma.

"Excuse me but I said that I have a friend coming so you will have to leave…now." *This is the problem with bars. There is always that one drunk old enough to be your father and yet they still try to pick you up.*

"Aw c'mon, pretty lady. Let me buy you a drink." Another obnoxiously loud hiccup and then he leaned over the table towards Quinn, trying to take her hand, which she promptly pulled away and in turn spilled her beer all over the table.

"Oh my God!" Jumping up out of the booth, Quinn grabbed her napkin and started mopping up the table and seat as best she could. "I think you better leave right now."

Leaning over the table to clean up the spill, she unexpectedly felt a hand squeeze her butt. Jumping up to attention, she gave a shocked look at the man.

"What the hell do you think you're doing?!" She shouted.

"Just 'copping a feel' pretty lady," the man slurred.

"Yeah, well, keep your hands off my ass and take *your* sorry drunken ass out of that booth or I'll be sure you never 'cop a feel' with that hand again!" Quinn was livid and now regretted arriving early.

Standing up, the drunk unsteadily stepped towards her and wrapped his arms around her waist. To her shock, he leaned in and tried to give her a slobbery drunken kiss, tripped and fell forward onto her, sending Quinn back onto the bench of the booth, with him right on top of her.

Pushing him off, Quinn quickly stood back up. The stranger took the opportunity to try once again to kiss her. She couldn't believe what was happening and tried to fend him off once more, with no success. She was amazed no one was noticing the difficulty she was having but the music and the crowd were loud.

Seeing no other alternative, Quinn grabbed her beer bottle and hit him over the head with it, sending him stumbling backwards against the bar, only a few yards away, and into the people sitting there, who didn't take kindly to being landed on by a drunken old man.

It was around this time the bartender finally noticed what was going on and with that, signalled the bouncer to come over to deal with things.

"Oh good, you're here," she said as the bouncer approached her.

"You have to leave." The bouncer stood right in front of her with his arms crossed.

"What?! Why do *I* have to leave?" Quinn was incredulous. She thought he was coming to help her, not kick her out.

"You're causing trouble and you need to leave…now."

"*I'm* causing trouble! *I'm* not the one causing trouble. This drunken old man here is the one causing trouble!"

With a hiccup, the drunk interjected, "Now, wait just a minute." Another hiccup.

Looking in the direction of the old man, Quinn rolled her eyes.

"You need to leave now." The bouncer's voice grew more stern.

"I will *not* leave! I didn't do anything wrong! I absolutely will not leave!"

With that, the bouncer grabbed her by the arm and began to escort her towards the door. As she tried to pull her arm up out of his iron-clad grip, she accidentally hit him in the face with her elbow and that was the beginning of the end for her. It was then that the bouncer pulled out his cellphone, made a call and within minutes the police arrived. After speaking privately with them, the security guard left the police to deal with Quinn.

"So, we understand you hit a guy over the head with a beer bottle…"

"But officer I was being harassed…"

"…and you assaulted the security guard." The police officer towered over Quinn as he spoke. "You know you can't do that, Lady."

Frowning, Quinn grew frustrated as she defended her case. "Yes, of course I know I can't do that, and I didn't…well, I did, but it wasn't like that. I was defending myself."

"Doesn't sound like that, according to security."

"Security didn't even give me a chance to explain."

"So, explain." The officer appeared bored.

After explaining what happened Quinn hoped for a reprieve and waited patiently.

"Okay, well, I'm willing to let this go, however, you still have to leave."

"Why?" Quinn was confused.

"Because the security guard said you can't stay."

"Did you not hear a word I said?"

"Yes, I heard every word you said, however, security was very clear that you need to leave."

"Even after what I just told you?"

"Yup. So, off you go, now." Quinn could see the indifference in the officer's face.

Quinn was incensed by the condescending manner of the officer.

"No."

"Pardon me?" The officer raised his eyebrows as he responded.

"I said, no. I don't think I should have to." Quinn was determined to stand her ground.

"Listen Lady, I suggest you leave while you're ahead." The officer grew more interested in the conversation.

"But, why should I leave? I didn't do anything wrong."

"Out." The officer pointed towards the front door.

Growing angrier by the second, Quinn felt this was one of those moments that she should stand up and defend, what she believed to be, fairness.

"No. I won't leave. I shouldn't have to leave and I won't leave. That drunken idiot should have to go, not me!" Quinn crossed her arms and refused to move.

"Listen Lady, you've picked the wrong night to piss me off. You either leave on your own accord or I take you into the station, but one way or the other, you're leaving. I'd rather not have to do the paperwork but I will if you force me to."

"Well…" Quinn hesitated before continuing. "…well, I'm not leaving." Inside, Quinn grew nervous. She decided to stand her ground, right here, right now and even though she didn't believe for a moment that he would take her to jail she was nervous just the same.

Shaking his head the officer, said, "Aw, shit!" Pulling out his handcuffs he added, "Fine. Have it your way, then." Putting the handcuffs on her, the officer continued, "I'm arresting you for failure to leave the premises when directed."

Panicking, Quinn was shocked by the turn of events. She honestly hadn't believed he would arrest her. She thought he was just trying to scare her.

"I don't understand how this could be happening! I didn't do anything wrong! I'm the victim here! I was the one accosted by that drunken old man! He grabbed my ass for chrissakes! I was trying to defend myself." She pleaded upon deaf ears as she was escorted out the door.

As the police officer shoved her into the back of the cruiser, he offered her some advice.

"If I were you, Lady, I wouldn't say another word. When you get to the station you can call someone to bail you out but in the meantime you're going to be spending some time in a jail cell."

"WHAT!?"

EIGHT

itting in the jail cell waiting to make her one phone call, Quinn heard her cellphone ringing in her purse on the counter near the officer in charge. He had been writing up a report and was ignoring the fact that the phone was ringing.

"Can I answer that? It could be my date looking for me. I don't want him to worry."

"No lady, you can't answer that. What part of 'you're in jail' don't you get?" The officer responded with disinterest shaking his head. "It's going into the lock-up with all your other belongings."

"Please. I don't have his number to call him."

"Too bad for you, Lady. You should have thought of that before you assaulted the bouncer." The officer was unsympathetic.

"But he'll worry that something terrible has happened to me," she pleaded.

"Something terrible *has* happened to you." He mundanely responded as he continued writing his report.

"You can consider it my one phone call," Quinn begged again.

Rolling his eyes, the officer thought about it then grabbed her phone, looked it over and handed it to her through the cell bars. "Make it quick and no funny business."

By then the phone had stopped ringing but Quinn took a chance and redialed the number that had just called hoping it would be Darcy.

Picking it up, Darcy immediately asked, "Quinn? Is that you? Where are you? I can't find you in the bar."

Hearing the music blaring in the background, Quinn spoke loudly into the phone, "Hi, Darcy, I um…listen, it's a long story and I can't talk long but I have a favour to ask of you."

"Sure, is everything okay?" Darcy could hear the distress in her voice.

"Well, when I was waiting for you at the Beagle at Bay, I got into a fight with a drunk and they threw me in jail."

There was silence at the other end of the phone.

"Darcy?"

"You what? I can't hear you very well." Darcy shouted into the phone. "It sounded like you said you were in jail."

"Yes, I was accosted by a drunk and hit the bouncer, well, I didn't mean to hit the bouncer, it was an accident…"

"Hurry up, Lady. You're running out of time," the officer warned.

Looking at the officer, Quinn grew concerned and spoke faster, "I'm in jail at…" Thinking for a moment she asked, "What station am I at?"

"Twenty-seven," the officer replied, clearly bored with his report writing.

"…at Station twenty-seven and I only get one phone call and this is it. Can you come bail me out?" Quinn asked in desperation.

In disbelief, Darcy was almost laughing as he spoke, "So, just to clarify. You *are* in jail, then?"

"Yes, I'm in jail."

"And you need me to come and bail you out…"

"Lady, you have about thirty-seconds to wrap it up." The officer now stood staring at her, tapping his finger on his watch.

Nodding, she scowled when she heard laughter at the other end of the phone.

"It's not *that* funny! In fact, it's not funny at all!"

"Okay, okay. I'll be right there." Darcy was still laughing when he hung up.

Handing her phone back to the officer, Quinn thought how she would have preferred to call François but since this was to be her only phone call, she hung up knowing it was out of the question to call him. As humiliating as it was to ask Darcy to come get her, she knew that he was her only hope at the moment.

• ● •

It felt like forever before she heard Darcy's voice speaking with the officer in charge before hearing the officer tell him to wait where he was and he would get the prisoner.

Oh my God, I'm a prisoner. Quinn was mortified hearing those words.

Unlocking the cell door, the officer said, "Now listen young lady, you can't go around assaulting people at bars nor can you refuse to leave when an officer tells you to. You'd be wise to remember that next time you lose your temper."

"But I was defend…" Quinn began but seeing the warning look on the officer's face, she knew this wasn't the time to voice her objections. Retrieving her belongings, Quinn walked out to the front waiting area and was surprisingly relieved to see Darcy, who immediately laughed at the sight of her.

"You look a mess!" he kindly shared.

"Gee, thanks." Quinn shook her head and walked out the door ahead of him.

"Soooo…what happened?" Darcy grinned. "They said you hit a guy in the bar, assaulted a bouncer, then refused when a police officer asked you to leave?" He waited a moment but she remained silent.

"You know you shouldn't do that, right?" He was purposely teasing her but couldn't help himself.

"Yes, I know that! It wasn't my fault!" With that, Quinn explained to Darcy exactly what happened.

"Worst...night...ever!" she finished off.

"Well, I must admit, this isn't exactly the best first date I've ever had but it's certainly the most interesting." Darcy was finding it hard to contain his laughter. He found the entire scenario hilarious. "I know it's late but would you still like to go out for dinner? That is, of course, if you can keep your hands to yourself."

"Ha! Ha! Ha! No thanks! I've had enough of being out for one night. I really appreciate you bailing me out though and I will pay you back but can you just take me home?"

Once in his car Darcy decided to add to her misery. "You do realize that you've been banned from the Beagle at Bay for a year."

"Really?" Quinn was surprised at the news though she was too tired to really care all that much.

"And you were actually arrested for causing a disturbance in a public place and not leaving when directed but I managed to get you released unconditionally with no charges, therefore, no bail required providing you adhere to the ban." Seeing Quinn silently nod as he spoke, Darcy continued, "...however, you do owe me for your bar bill."

"Really? Oh my God, it's just mortifying...the whole scenario. I just can't believe it happened at all."

"I'll take you to pick up your car."

"Oh, right, my car. Am I at least allowed in the parking lot of the Beagle at Bay?"

Laughing, Darcy assured her that, by all means, she could retrieve her car from the parking lot.

Resting her head back against the headrest Quinn closed her eyes momentarily. She suddenly felt exhausted.

"Darcy, after we get my car would you like to come back to my place for a bite to eat? We could order pizza. I have wine and beer. I'm starving and it's the least I could do since you got me out of jail."

"Works for me. I could use a beer right about now."

• ● •

Back at her condo, Quinn finished her pizza. Settling into the easy chair, she put her feet up onto the coffee table and sipped on her wine. She was finally relaxing after her ridiculously eventful evening.

"This is the first time I've ever been arrested."

"You don't say." Darcy grinned.

"Yup, and I must admit, I feel rather badass!" she laughed.

"I must admit you're more badass than I gave you credit for. Darcy was trying to contain his laughter as he added insult to injury, "Oh, by the way, here's the bar bill."

Frowning, she reluctantly reached for it, "How much do I owe you?"

Looking at it she instantly grew angry. "Are you kidding me? They charged me for the old man's bar bill too?!"

NINE

"**A**RRESTED!?" François was shocked at Quinn's announcement when they met for breakfast the following day at Dills and Dolls. The place was busy as per usual on a Saturday.

"Shhhh, François! I don't need the entire place hearing." Quinn self-consciously looked around to see if anyone was paying attention to their conversation.

Lowering his voice, François asked, "What the hell happened on this date of yours that you ended up in jail?"

Listening to Quinn explain what took place the night before, François cried he was laughing so hard by the end of the story.

"...and Darcy got you out? Oh my God, Q, that's hilarious! Talk about your bad first impression...okay second impression."

"Yeah, hilarious for you and hilarious for Darcy. Not so much for me!" she lamented knowing that her friend wouldn't let her forget about this for a very long time.

"Are you going to have a record?" François was curious.

"No, thank goodness. Darcy managed to get me off unconditionally."

"And you're not allowed back at the Beagle at Bay for a year?!"

"According to Darcy, I'm not."

"Oh my God, you do manage to get yourself into some crazy predicaments, Q!"

"Yeah but, do you really think they would remember me if I went there?" Quinn contemplated the possibility.

"Let's just say I wouldn't risk it…unless you want to go back in the slammer again, that is."

Quinn rolled her eyes then took another sip of her latte without dignifying François with a response.

"So when are you and Darcy going on another date?" François was more than interested. "Or did you scare him off after last night's misadventure?" He quizzed. "Did he stay overnight?" Knowing his friend, he figured as much.

"No he did not! Are you crazy? After the night I had?" Quinn was surprisingly indignant.

François was taken aback by her response, so uncharacteristic of his friend since she left Spencer. *She really does like him.* He knew that there was something about this guy that intrigued Q. *This sounds rather promising.*

"I told you that I'm not interested in him. Besides, what kind of guy would even *want* to see me again after last night? What would that tell you about his state of mind?"

Quinn mulled that thought over for a moment then added, "Anyway, I'm not entirely sure he *is* of sound mind because we are going out tonight…" Seeing the hopeful look on her friend's face, Quinn qualified her comment, "…but *only* because this is still technically our first date," she offered defensively.

"Oh…yeah…I get it." François smirked.

Quinn gave her friend a dirty look.

"This time, he said he is going to pick me up until, as he put it… I learn to keep my hands to myself." Quinn turned to her friend with a deadpan look on her face. François couldn't help but laugh at her expense.

"Oh, shut up, François!"

TEN

"**T**hanks for picking me up, Darcy."

"Well, I must say it's kind of nice not to have to pick you up from a police station this time," he teased.

"Yeah, I suppose it's all fun and games until you need to bail out your date, isn't it?" Quinn chuckled as she locked her condo door behind them. "So where are we going?"

"Ah, as far away from a bar as we can get."

Although she would never have admitted it, Quinn was rather curious as to what he had in mind. After a half hour drive they arrived at their destination, a high-rise office building in the downtown core of the city.

"Here we are." Darcy parked underground and getting out of the car, walked around and opened Quinn's door. "Grab your coat."

Following him through the parking garage to an elevator, Quinn was quite interested to know where Darcy was taking her.

"Isn't this the Monaghan's Outdoor World building? I've been down this way many times but don't remember any restaurants nearby."

"There aren't any." Darcy smiled. "Only here in the building but it's closed for the day."

"But I don't understand. I thought we were having dinner."

"We are."

Following Darcy, Quinn stepped into the elevator and watched as he hit the button that would take them to the top floor. Stepping out on the 39th floor, they continued down a long corridor to a door marked 'Stairs to Roof'. Walking up two more flights of stairs, Quinn wondered what Darcy was up to and in the back of her mind began to wonder if she was, in fact, dating a serial killer, who was about to do away with her off the roof. *I mean, seriously, what do I really know about this guy, anyway?*

Walking through the door to the roof, Quinn felt a cool breeze brush her face and followed Darcy around some large metal ductwork where her worries immediately disappeared.

Stopping, Quinn inhaled quickly. "Oh my God. This is…" Tears came to her eyes and she had to quickly gain control. "…this is so beautiful." She whispered the words as she spoke.

In front of her was an area set up with a portable fire pit, a couple of camp chairs, side table, patio lanterns everywhere and a bottle of something chilling in a portable cooler.

"Darcy…" Quinn was emotional. No one had ever done anything like this for her before. Her heart melted at the sight.

"Come sit down and I'll light the fire. It's a bit chilly with the breeze up here."

Quinn slowly walked over and sat down on one of the foldable camp chairs while Darcy lit the fire. She noticed that the chairs, fire pit and cooler all had the Monaghan Outdoor World logo on them. Darcy had clearly thought of everything. There was even a stack of wood ready when needed. She had to admit that the warmth of the fire was welcome.

"Here, I brought these just in case." Darcy placed a small blanket over Quinn's legs. "Do you want some wine?"

"Umm, okay sure, that would be nice, thanks." Quinn smiled nervously as she watched Darcy open the bottle of wine and pour them each a glass. Trying to think of something to say, she accepted her drink and smiled awkwardly.

"I love the fancy glasses. The red plastic beer cup seems perfect for the occasion."

"I thought so." Darcy smiled and held his cup up and tapped it gently to Quinn's who immediately took a sip.

Quinn felt strangely nervous.

"I brought dinner. I think you'll like it."

Quinn was staring at the fire when she was surprised to be handed a long wire fork.

"What the…?"

"Oh and you'll need these to go with that."

"Hot dogs?" Quinn laughed.

Stopping to look at her with concern, Darcy asked, "You don't like hot dogs?"

Smiling, Quinn responded. "No…I love hot dogs!" Opening up the package Quinn grabbed one and placed it on her fork. "Would you like me to cook one up for you as well?"

"That would be great, thank you!"

Adding a second hot dog, Quinn began to cook them over the fire. *Well, well, Darcy, you are a surprise. This couldn't be more perfect.* Her nervousness subsided.

"I have some fresh buns, mustard, relish, ketchup and some potato chips to finish the main dish off nicely. And for the health conscious in you, some fresh veggies." She watched as Darcy pulled all the food out and placed it on the table between them.

Several minutes later, sitting back enjoying her hot dog and wine, Quinn felt more relaxed and content than she had in years. To her, this was the perfect date. Relaxing by an open fire, stars shining brightly overhead, a full moon and enjoying the beautiful city skyline with a guy who was surprisingly winning over her heart. In the distance she could hear the slight rumble of the traffic below, horns honking, sirens sounding.

"So Darcy, where did you grow up?" Quinn wanted to know more about this intriguing man.

"Well, I grew up in the city here. My parents were from Scotland. Edinburgh to be exact, and when I was nine they decided to move here and set up house. My sisters were eleven and six at the time but my older sister died shortly after moving here…"

"I'm so sorry. What happened?"

"She caught pneumonia. My parents, being new here, had no insurance so were unable to afford any hospital bills and they tried to care for her at home themselves. Needless to say, that didn't work out. My mother was devastated and could barely function for years after and spent most of her time staying at home and sleeping. I remember every morning after my father left for work he would drop my younger sister off at school. I went to a different school and before catching the school bus, I would get my own breakfast, make my own lunch and then go into my parents bedroom to kiss my mother good-bye. Then one morning, my father didn't go into work and said he needed to take my mother to hospital. I went into the bedroom to see her and she hugged me tighter than usual and told me she had to go to the hospital for a little while, said how much she loved me, to take care of my sister and to always be a good boy. My father came to get me from school later that day and told me she had died at hospital. People said she died of heartbreak. I later found out it was cancer."

"Oh my God, Darcy. That's terrible!"

"Oh hey, listen, I'm not trying to bring down the evening here. Life goes on and my Pop, sister and I moved from that house in the suburbs of Lancaster to downtown here. He met a beautifully sweet woman who he eventually married. They are still happily married after 25 years. She's kind and life is good. Naturally, I missed my mother…still do, but Kathleen is such a wonderful person and has been a wonderful mother to me and my sister."

Quietly contemplative, they sat staring at the fire.

"So, enough about me, tell me about you. Brothers? Sisters? Evil stepmother?" Darcy laughed. Pouring them more wine he added wood to the fire.

Quinn took in a deep breath, enjoying the smell of the wood burning.

"Pretty mundane really. Mother, father, one sister, grandmother. Not close to any of them except for my grandmother. Grew up in the burbs as well. A few years after college I met a boy…well, actually my parents introduced us and I thought that I fell madly in love…" Quinn became very quiet. "…we were actually engaged to be married."

Looking over at her, Darcy noticed tears in her eyes. "Didn't work out, huh?"

"Well, you could say that."

Darcy said nothing, waiting for Quinn to continue

"So, Darcy, I have to say, this is one of the best dates I've ever been on. It's been awhile since I sat around a campfire. I used to love them at my grandparents' cabin in the mountains."

"Used to?" Darcy was curious.

"Well, my grandfather died a couple of years ago. My grandmother still lives there but now when I go there, it isn't so much for campfires as it is to help my grandmother with whatever she can't manage on her own. It's a hundred year old cabin that my grandfather bought about thirty years ago and they retired to. I used to go up there every summer as a little girl. I loved it there. It was the best place to go and have some fun and freedom. Unfortunately, my grandmother is in her eighties now and can't do everything she used to, although she's still pretty spry for her age. She refuses to leave. Says she's going to die there. My parents and sister hate the place and have always wanted her to sell it and move closer to them. She pretty much told them to shove it." She laughed at the thought.

Suddenly realizing she had said too much, Quinn said no more. Grabbing another hot dog she began cooking it over the fire.

Changing the subject, she asked, "So how come security isn't running up here chasing us away? I mean, I can't imagine you received permission to have a fire up here. That's gotta be breaking a few fire regulations." Quinn laughed and placed her puffed up hot dog into a bun and carefully squirted mustard on top.

"Well, I have a few connections." Darcy said quietly.

"I must admit, you've thought of everything. I'm impressed."

"Ah, but there is one more surprise I have for you…" Darcy reached into the cooler sitting beside him. "Dessert." He smiled as he showed Quinn what he had.

"Oh my God, Darcy! I love s'mores! I haven't had s'mores since I was a little girl. You really did think of everything!" Quinn was quickly falling for this man. It made her uneasy but she was trying to just 'be happy and enjoy life for a change' as François had so annoyingly put it far too many times for her liking.

A few minutes later she had finished her hot dog and was savouring the s'more Darcy had made for her. Throwing a few more pieces of wood on the fire, Darcy topped up their wine and sat back in his chair, crossing his legs on a stray piece of wood waiting to be burned.

Taking a deep breath in and then out again, Quinn closed her eyes and enjoyed the warmth and smell of the fire for a few quiet moments.

"Darcy, do you ever wish you could stay right where you are forever?"

Staring into the fire, Darcy nodded his head, "Yeah. There have been times, I must admit."

Eyes still closed, Quinn smiled to herself, "Me too." Opening her eyes again she was transfixed by the fire. "This is one of those moments for me," she said quietly, more to herself than to Darcy. "Thank you." She almost whispered the words.

Saying nothing, Darcy just smiled. He loved how honestly Quinn spoke about things. There was nothing pretentious about her. After a few minutes he asked, "Well, are you up for another s'more?"

Laughing, Quinn nodded her head with approval, "I sure am!"

ELEVEN

Shivering, Quinn grabbed the fleece blanket Darcy had brought and wrapped it around her shoulders.

"What time is it anyway?" Pulling out her phone she exclaimed, "Wow, it's just after midnight. Boy, did that time ever go by fast. Thank you so much, Darcy. I've had such a wonderful evening."

"Getting cold?" Darcy poked the fire a few times. "The fire is starting to die down. I have a couple more pieces of wood left, shall I throw them on?"

"Absolutely, please do! I'm not ready to leave just yet." Truer words had never been spoken for Quinn.

"I have one more beer if you are interested. I can't have it because I'm driving," he offered.

"Sure why not? I can't believe we finished the wine and the beer, not to mention having dogs and s'mores."

Just then the roof door flew open and a security guard quickly marched towards them.

Quinn immediately sat up and anxiously awaited what would inevitably be nothing but trouble. *Well, that's the end of our lovely evening. With my luck I'll be going back to jail again tonight.*

"Hey there! You people! What are you two doing up here? You're trespassing and must leave immedi…" Stopping in his tracks, the security guard added, "Oh, Mr. M., I'm sorry I didn't realize it was you up here."

"That's okay, Warren, I'm happy to see you're right on it." Darcy smiled without getting up from his chair.

Hesitating, the guard offered, "Okay…okay then. Well, Marvin became ill and I am filling in the remainder of his shift for him. He failed to mention you would be here."

"That's quite alright, Warren," Darcy reassured the anxious guard.

"Okay…okay then…" Thinking carefully for a moment, Warren felt obliged to continue, "You do realize that it's against fire regulations to have a fire on the roof, Sir."

Chuckling, Darcy said, "I do know that, yes, Warren, but thank you for the reminder."

Hesitating once again, Warren said, "Okay…okay then…well, I'll carry on with my rounds." Thinking for a moment he added, "Just remember to put that fire out completely, sir."

"I will Warren."

"Okay…okay then…I'm sorry to disturb you." Starting to slowly back away, Warren added, "Again, I'm…I'm very sorry for the interruption, Mr. M." With that, he turned around and quickly left through the same door he came rushing through moments earlier.

Quinn was speechless. Her mouth dropped open not sure what to say about the scene that just unfolded.

"Sorry about that." Darcy poked the fire one last time then sat back and relaxed in his chair once again.

When Quinn finally found her words, she asked, "What was that all about?"

"That was security guard Warren Trapman doing his job. One of the best there is."

"But, why was he calling you Mr. M.?" Quinn was starting to put the pieces of the puzzle together but didn't want to ask the direct question.

"Well, he doesn't really have to call me Mr. M., or Sir for that matter. I've told him many times just to call me Darcy but he can't seem to bring himself to do it. Mr. M. is as casual as it gets with him." Darcy shook his head and chuckled.

"But I'm a bit confused. Do you actually work here?"

"Yes, I definitely work here."

"What do you do?

"I'm the COO. The Chief Operating Officer."

"Oh." Quinn looked at Darcy as he stared at the fire.

"My dad's the CEO, Chief Executive Officer."

"Really…" Quinn's mouth dropped open.

"My mom's CFO, the Chief Financial Officer."

"Really? Wow! Okay…that's pretty impressive." She was more amazed with each word he spoke. *Who the heck are these people?*

"And your sister?"

"Well, she's a different story. She started her own business, well, a couple of them, but does sit on the board of directors…"

"Really?" Quinn knew she was repeating herself but couldn't help it.

"…as Chairman of the Board."

Raising her eyebrows in surprise, Quinn responded, "Really?!" Thinking for a moment she added, "Talk about keeping it all in the family." Quinn was completely dumbfounded. "The only thing that could surprise me more is if you said you and your family were *actually* the Monaghans of Monaghan's Outdoor World and that you owned the place."

"Oh, I am…"

"What?" Quinn looked up, shocked.

"And, we are…" Darcy said matter-of-factly.

"Really?"

"…and, we do," he finished up.

Stopping cold, Quinn looked with amazement at Darcy.

"You're kidding…right?"

"Ummm…nope."

"Seriously?"

"Ummm…yup."

"Well, okay, then." Quinn wasn't sure what else to say. There *was* nothing more to say. It was at this moment that she and Darcy looked at each other and burst out laughing.

Handing Quinn the beer he had previously offered, he added, "Good thing Warren didn't see us with the beer or wine. He would have completely gone over the edge." Laughing, he added, "He's our best security guard, follows the rules so it was hard enough for him to see the fire here but add alcohol to the mix and that would have just about done it for him."

Quinn laughed hearing this. "I can only imagine."

"Don't get me wrong, I have a great deal of respect for him and there's no better security guard in my opinion. He's worked for us since he graduated ten years ago. He's now assistant head of security and he's earned it. A fire on the roof is completely forbidden so you can imagine how badly he was itching to kick us off this roof just now or at the very least throw some water on the fire." Darcy said, laughing.

Smiling, Quinn looked over as Darcy poked what was left of the fire. *He really is quite a surprise.*

Having talked until the fire was completely done, Quinn thought about how she hadn't felt this relaxed on a date in a very long time. *If it wasn't absolutely crazy, I would say I've already fallen in love with this man but of course I couldn't have now, could I? I mean, that would be completely ludicrous. No one falls in love that quickly, especially me. I*

*don't even know him and God knows I have no interest in getting serious
with anyone…*

"Quinn?"

"Oh, yes Darcy, I'm sorry, what did you say?" She realized that he had
been speaking to her and she hadn't heard a word he had said.

"I just asked if you were ready to go now?"

"Oh, sure. What time is it?"

"It's after two in the morning."

"Wow! Yes, absolutely. I suppose it's getting a bit too chilly to stay now
that all the wood is gone, anyway."

"Here grab this chair will you? I'll throw everything in my trunk so
Warren doesn't have to do any explaining to the next guard on shift.
The fire pit stays up here. It's too hot to move anyway. I'll get it later."
Darcy laughed as he poured a bottle of water onto the embers, then
handed Quinn both of the folded-up chairs as he grabbed the table and
the cooler on wheels.

Arriving in front of her building, Quinn realized she didn't want the
night to end.

"Darcy, why don't you…well, would you like to…" Quinn started to
get tongue-tied which was not typical for her. "Oh, dammit, would you
like to come up for a coffee? I'm not tired and I have nowhere to be
tomorrow…that is, of course, if you would like to…"

"Yeah, sure." Darcy agreed quickly.

Relieved, Quinn said, "Okay…good, that would be…that would be
great, then." She smiled to herself as she got out of the car.

TWELVE

*Q*uinn awoke the next morning to frantic knocking on her door and scrambled to answer it. Opening it up, she sighed and headed into the kitchen.

"What the hell are you doing knocking on my door at…" Pausing, Quinn turned to look at François. "What the hell time is it?"

"It's one o'clock, Q, and we are supposed to go to the Red Bulb Fashion Show today, remember?"

"Why didn't you just use your key to get in instead of banging on my door so loudly?" Giving her head a rub with her hand, Quinn ruffled her hair trying to wake herself up.

"Because I forgot it in my car. Why aren't you ready?" François asked.

"I'm sorry, François, I forgot all about it. Want a coffee?" She filled the coffeemaker with water and ground some coffee beans, carefully pouring them into the coffeemaker for brewing.

"You look like hell." François couldn't help but notice the smudged mascara under his best friend's eyes and her hair was a complete mess. She looked like she hadn't slept all night.

"Gee, thanks," she muttered.

"What time did you get to bed last night? How did your date go with…" François suddenly stopped talking and his mouth dropped open.

"Ummm, never mind, Sweetheart…I guess it went very well…" he said as his voice trailed off.

Quinn looked up to see why he had stopped talking. Following his gaze towards the hall she fully comprehended François' more than curious interest and bit down on her bottom lip. They were both completely transfixed as they watched Darcy walk out of her bedroom, down the hall towards them in the kitchen. His dark brown hair seemed strategically disheveled. Shirt in hand, he was wearing nothing but his skin-tight jeans, which only helped to emphasize his obviously fit physique. Walking barefoot and looking adorably sleepy, Darcy had that five o'clock shadow that most men would have paid to have look so perfect and sexy.

Heart racing, Quinn had to admit she was more than turned on at that moment and completely mesmerized by the sight of him. Still biting down on her lip Quinn thought, *Oh...my...God, he's hot!*

Speaking quietly, François said, "Well, I must say, Quinn, I can understand why you forgot about the fashion show. My God!"

"Yeah..." Quinn's voice drifted off as she continued to stare.

"Oh, hey, you must be François. We didn't get a chance to formally meet at the wedding. I'm Darcy. How's it going?" Shaking hands with François, Darcy wasn't at all surprised to see him standing in Quinn's kitchen at that moment. He knew they had been friends for a very long time.

"Pleasure." François' voice was barely audible as he shook Darcy's hand. Quinn raised her eyebrows and chuckled as she watched her friend swooning, not that she could blame him.

THIRTEEN

*M*onday arrived and Quinn couldn't have been happier. The day was nothing but blue skies and sunshine, making her condo feel warm and cozy. Leaves had slowly started falling off trees and the crispness of fall was replacing the warmer than usual late October temperatures.

I love nothing better than a day like today. I'm so grateful I can just relax. Remembering her weekend with Darcy, Quinn smiled. She felt genuinely happy for the first time in years. *Not that it will last but even so, I can't deny it will be fun while it does.*

Trundling out of her bedroom in her pajamas and sock covered feet, Quinn made a coffee, curled up on the couch in the living room and stared out the window. Daydreaming about what the future could bring with Darcy, she quickly shook all thoughts away reminding herself that this was just a fling like all the others, although deep down she knew this might not be true. Even she had to admit to herself that Darcy was nothing like the others and more importantly, nothing like Spencer. Putting on some music, Quinn finished her coffee then quickly ate breakfast. She had some errands to run and didn't want to head out too late.

Brushing her teeth, she heard the phone ring and quickly spit out the toothpaste, threw her brush down and ran to pick it up.

"Hello?"

"Quinn, it's your mother calling."

"Oh, hello, Mother." Quinn was less than enthusiastic and silently scolded herself for not checking the call display on her phone before answering.

"I just spoke to François and he said you were in jail! Somehow, I always knew it would come to this with you!"

I'm going to kill that little French bastard!

"You called François about me? Why would you do that, Mother, and what do you mean, somehow you always knew it would come to this? What are you implying?"

"I was having a fitting done for the clothes I just purchased. Why else would I be speaking to him? Why were you in jail? Your father is furious to say the least."

"Mother, it was nothing, just a misunderstanding."

Sighing, her mother continued, "If it's not one thing, it's another with you, Quinn. What are your father and I ever going to do about you? For God's sake, it's disgusting the way you live. Getting thrown in jail, living in some low rent rooming house, sleeping with every man you meet. What has gotten into you these days?"

Damn, François! That Frenchman has too big of a mouth for his own good, and mine!

"It's a condo, Mother, and I don't sleep with every man I meet. Why are you calling? What do you want?"

"Condominium then, but it's in a rather undesirable part of the city. God knows what questionable types are lurking about there…"

"It's in the theatre district, Mother. It's not undesirable, it's actually quite a sought-after area, and there is no one lurking about. Honestly, Mother! You are one of the most patronizing individuals I know. What do you want?"

"I am most certainly *not* patronizing. People of our status don't live in undesirable areas, do not get thrown into jail and God knows, we don't sleep with every person…"

"Mother, why are you calling?" Quinn grew frustrated.

"Your father and I just don't understand you at all."

So what else is new?

"Why aren't you more like your sister, Madison?"

Quinn rolled her eyes.

"Did you know she's doing volunteer work now? She's a very independent woman."

"Mother, Madison's idea of volunteer work is arranging dinner parties at the club for Bradley's law firm colleagues. That is not volunteer work and you really do need to learn what independence is all about. I can assure you it has nothing to do with you and daddy constantly handing out money to Madison and her fiancé."

There was silence at the other end of the phone. Quinn could only hope that a dial tone would follow but she had no such luck.

"With Madison now getting married, you know that your father will want to speak to you about settling down, Quinn. God knows you completely made a mess of that relationship with Spencer..."

"Wow, Mother! That's heartless!"

"Spencer was a wonderful young man and you had the chance of a lifetime to marry him..."

"That would have been a lifetime of misery had I married him! He's a cheating bastard and I know you don't understand it, but it isn't normal to cheat on your fiancée and I wasn't willing to accept that!" Quinn grew angrier than she had in a long time.

"Well, it's too late now." Her mother's voice faded as she spoke.

Quinn was trying not to cry and doing her best not to let her mother know that she had opened a wound that had just finally started healing. Composing herself, Quinn sternly asked, "Is that all, Mother? I need to go."

There was an awkward silence before her mother spoke once again.

Sighing, her mother asked, "Where did we ever go wrong with you?"

"Why would you say you went wrong, Mother?" Quinn choked back

HER *FLAW*SOME LIFE

the tears. She hated these conversations. They were part of the reason she moved away from her family home, to begin with.

"Your sister has never been thrown into jail; she has never had multiple men in her life. She is a member of the Emerald Club where she will soon marry Bradley Archer, who, by the way, will soon be partner at the law firm…"

"Father's law firm…" Quinn didn't even try to hide the sarcasm.

"It doesn't matter whose law firm. He is very suitable for the family."

Never mind whether he's suitable for Madison.

"The fact of the matter is, that Madison has always conducted herself appropriately but not you, no, you have rebelled every step of the way. I thought you would have grown up by now…"

"Well thank you for that, Mother. Are we done?"

Exasperated, Quinn's mother replied, "Yes, I suppose we are. Good Lord, Quinn, we can never have a conversation without an argument."

"Perhaps we could have just one conversation where you didn't tell me what a disappointment I am!" Quinn blurted out the words.

"How dare you, Quinn! I have never said you were a disappointment."

"Maybe not in so many words but trust me it has always been implied. Is there anything else you would like to speak to me about, Mother? I'm busy." Quinn needed to get off the phone before she lost her mind completely.

"No, I suppose there isn't. God knows, conversations with you are never easy. "

There was an awkward silence and Quinn knew to say nothing or the conversation would continue.

"Well, fine then…I'll be sure to tell your father you said hello."

"Sure, you do that." Quinn resentfully spit the words out, but before hanging up, she needed to say one last thing.

"You know, Mother…" Quinn had difficulty controlling her emotions.

"What?" Her mother sounded exasperated and disinterested.

"It's a good 'ole boys club, Mother. The men can do whatever they want with no consequences but if the women dare deviate from what is expected of them, then there is hell to pay. Spencer is not the person he is made out to be. He cheated on me, Mother…". Choking back the tears, she continued.

"…he cheated on me. And not just with one woman but with multiple women. Everyone at the Emerald Club knew this, you and daddy knew this, Madison knew it and yet, no one said anything to me, not even you. You didn't even defend me, your own daughter. The cheating aside, I walked away from that relationship and that lifestyle because I was naive and I was foolish to ever think you would come to my defence and I needed to leave with what semblance of dignity I had left."

Slamming the phone down, tears were streaming down Quinn's cheeks.

"And he broke your little girl's heart but you don't care about that do you…?"

Just then the phone rang again. Not picking it up, Quinn listened as her mother left a message.

"Quinn I know you're there so you might just as well pick up…Quinn?"

Quinn could hear a heavy sigh followed by, "My God you need to stop being so emotional."

Naturally, that's what you take from everything I said. Quinn wiped away the tears.

"Your father and I are coming into the city in a few days. He has business to attend to. We are staying at the Queen's Hotel. We expect you to join us for dinner on Friday night at Smith's, the hotel restaurant. It's a high-end restaurant so be sure to dress appropriately…if you have anything that is. Since you managed to get yourself fired your father and I will pay for your meal…" And with that, her mother's message ended.

If you're coming into town, then I'm leaving.

Taking time to compose herself, Quinn got dressed then picked up the phone and dialled.

"Hello?"

"François, why the hell would you ever tell my mother I was thrown in jail? How could you?!"

"Absolutely! Just one moment and I'll go to my office and get that information for you."

"What?" Quinn was momentarily confused and then realized he was likely in a meeting when she called.

A few moments later, François almost whispered into the phone but his frustration was evident, "She bullied it out of me, Quinn. You know how she gets. She pushes until you get so exasperated that you give in and tell her whatever she wants to know. She's like a fucking interrogator! She…NEVER…LET'S…UP!" François' voice became louder the more he spoke.

Chuckling to herself, she could only imagine how that conversation went and took pity on her friend.

"And for the record, I didn't tell her. Apparently, the Staff Sergeant on duty that night knows your father because your father is his lawyer and *he* told your father you were in jail."

"Are you kidding me?" Quinn couldn't believe what she was hearing. "What ever happened to confidentiality?" It was a rhetorical question because her parents' 'tentacles' reached far and she knew it. "My God! I can't even get arrested without my parents finding out!"

Sighing loudly, he asked, "How in hell did you ever survive your childhood with that fucking woman?!"

Laughing, Quinn said, "Okay, okay, fair enough. I know what she's like."

"Oh, I don't think you really do. Try doing business with her. She's constantly bartering price, materials, sizing…"

François was clearly frustrated and Quinn sympathized.

"Do you realize that your mother has me change the sizing on her clothing so that people think she wears a smaller size? That there isn't one piece of clothing that she has purchased from us that hasn't had the price bartered? My God, Q, you have no idea what I deal with on a regular basis."

François was irritated and Quinn knew not to push him any further.

"I just wanted to let you know I'm skipping town in a few days. My parents are coming into the city and they want to have dinner with me…"

"Oh, fuck no!"

"Yeah, I know, right? So, can you get some time off and come with me?" Quinn was doubtful, yet hopeful.

"No, are you kidding me? It's too busy around here right now. We are starting preparations for our Spring show and that fucking bitch Monica walked out on us today."

"Monica? But she's your top model! Why? You all went to school together, you're partners. I thought that this was an 'all in for the long haul' or 'no one in' scenario when you opened shop together."

"Well, Fayeed and I thought so too but the little traitor got a job in New York City with Sparks & Brown Designs."

"Really?! Wow! Aren't they one of the top designers?"

"They are. What of it?"

Did I catch a hint of defensiveness? Quinn wasn't sure.

"Didn't you tell me that it's hard to even get in for an interview with them, let alone a job? Is she modelling for them?"

"Yes and yes, dammit!"

"How…?"

"God knows!" François sighed. "She likely slept her way through the interview process."

"François! What a nasty thing to say!"

"I'm sorry, Q. I clearly don't mean that...well, I suppose I do. Anyway, it's been a terrible day, between that and your fucking mother."

"You're preaching to the choir, my friend."

"I'm stressed to the max about our Spring show. It's the first one we actually have a complete line we are happy with and to have that bitch Monica walk out on us like this...well..." He seemed to go quiet all of a sudden, then added, "...well...it's extremely disappointing. We've worked so hard for this and as if it wasn't bad enough that Monica quit but now Fayeed wants to find a replacement so that we are up and running before the show. I say, good luck with that. God knows, Fayeed has no idea what it takes to replace someone in the fashion industry. He has never taken an interest in any of the business side of things. He's only been interested in the design aspect and now he wants to be in charge of finding a replacement?!" François vented.

"So why all of a sudden has he decided he wants to look after finding a replacement for Monica?" Quinn was confused.

"He says he has 'connections'...whatever the hell that means. My God, Fayeed's connections are usually less than reputable, however, he is an equal partner and quite frankly I'm just glad I don't have to take care of it. Christ, there's always someone out there who pays better, has a better office, more benefits and don't get me started on the fact that no one wants to work for an up and coming fashion designer these days. These kids come out of school with their noses still running and they expect to immediately hit the runways in Paris or New York with the Diors and Vuittons of the fashion world. The kids today have high expectations, no experience and their haughty attitudes could put me to shame! If Fayeed and I hadn't gone to school together and weren't such good friends, I'd quit myself. It's been a complete madhouse here today."

"Okay, then. Well, I guess I'm going on my own." She was disappointed. She always had fun with François but he was clearly stressed to the max and she didn't want to push him.

"Why not ask that ever so handsome Darcy to go with you?" François teased.

"No, we've been on one date. I don't know him well enough to go away with him. I don't even know if I want to date him again."

"Yes, okay, Quinn. As per usual, you're a commitment-phobe."

"I am not!" She barely believed herself.

"Oh, yes you are, and don't forget, we had a deal…of course, we can send you the designs to look at by the end of the day, Mrs. Smith. Well, I must go, I'm required in a meeting. Enjoy your time away and we will be in touch upon your return, Mrs. Smith." François' voice had become instantly professional.

"Don't be such a coward and tell Fayeed to go to hell, you can talk to whoever you want to on the phone. You're an equal partner for God's sake, remember?!" she tormented.

"Yes, I do and I would love to, Mrs. Smith, thank you." François responded truthfully.

"Okay, I'll say good-bye. Call me on my cell. We'll talk before I leave and good luck with the search."

"Yes, duly noted Mrs. Smith. Thank you and good-bye." And with that, François hung up the phone leaving Quinn chuckling.

Picking up the phone again, Quinn called her grandmother.

"Hello?" The familiar voice answered kindly. Quinn immediately smiled.

"Grandma? It's Quinn."

"Quinn! Oh my goodness, it's good to hear from you. How are you, Dear? I'm so pleased you called."

"I'm good! I was going to come up to visit you for a few days. Is that okay?"

"Absolutely! Come and stay longer if you want, that would be lovely. When are you going to head up?"

"I thought I would leave Friday morning and stay until Monday or Tuesday if you aren't busy."

"No plans at all. Oh and by the way, how is the job hunting going?"

"Not well, unfortunately." Quinn had to admit she was disappointed by the lack of job opportunities opening up.

"Are you sure you won't let me help you with some money just to tie you over?"

Unlike her parents, Quinn knew that her grandmother's offer came with no strings attached but she would never accept money from her, regardless.

"I'm fine Grandma. I got a great severance package. You don't need to worry about me. I'm just looking forward to seeing you. "

"It's been awhile since you've been here so it's just about time for a visit." Her grandmother teased.

"I can't wait!" Quinn was excited at the prospect of spending time with her grandmother.

"Your mother phoned me this morning. Honestly, that daughter of mine never changes. Always on about something and this time it was about you getting arrested? What happened? Are you alright?"

"Yes, it was a big misunderstanding and they let me go. I'll tell you all about it when I see you. It's actually kind of funny when I look back on it. I'm sure mother was flipping out, though."

Laughing, Esther said, "Oh, yes she was. Good thing your grandfather and I never told her about us being thrown in jail the time we were protesting animal rights."

"Really? You and Grandpa were arrested?" This was a story Quinn hadn't heard.

"Oh yes, Dear. In our younger days. More than once. Never for anything criminal, always during protests and then released unconditionally. I'll tell you more about it when you visit."

"Oh, I definitely want to hear all about it." Quinn was amazed at the insight she gained over the years from such stories about two of her favourite people. "Thank goodness I have you in my life. Everyone else has lost their minds." Quinn offered.

"Well, whatever you do, don't you ever borrow money from them. Always come to me. God knows you would be indebted for the rest of your life if you borrowed money from them."

"Don't worry, I won't." Quinn promised.

"Your father is a self-important pain in the ass and don't get me started about your mother. That upper class snobbery is exhausting to be around. I lose patience with the lot of them."

Quinn had never heard her grandmother speak quite so honestly about the family leading her to suspect that the conversation with her mother was much more than about Quinn's way of life.

"Now, enough about that. I'm so glad you are coming to the cabin. I miss you so much, Dear." Her grandmother's voice sounded a little emotional and there was silence at the other end of the phone for a moment.

"Anyway, you get yourself out here and let's have a girls' long weekend, just the two of us. The leaves have fallen up here. You can help me load some chopped wood onto the back porch for the fireplace. The nights are getting colder and I can tell you there is nowhere near enough wood for the winter."

Her grandmother was no slouch; always strong and independent. Something her grandfather said he loved about her. "She was always different from most girls of our generation, Quinn," he once told her. "Your grandmother was the tomboy in her group of friends and they never truly understood her but I loved her for it. I never did like all those helpless, needy female types." Quinn smiled at the little bit of insight her grandfather had periodically offered about the woman they both admired.

"Quinn? Are you there?"

Quinn realized she had been deep in thought and hadn't answered.

"Oh yes, I can't wait, Grandma! I love you! See you soon."

"I love you too, Dear."

Hanging up the phone, Quinn had a strong sense that something didn't feel quite right. She couldn't place it and expected it had something to do with the conversation her grandmother said she had with her mother. She decided that she would speak with her grandmother about this when she visited.

FOURTEEN

*L*ater that day, Quinn walked into Dills and Dolls, relieved Sasha wasn't there to hound her about yoga classes. She was a nice enough person but Quinn had no patience for someone who always saw the glass half full. It was infuriating. Seeing François sitting at their usual table, Quinn waved, grabbed a latte then sat down.

"So, have you heard from Darcy today?" François got down to business as soon as Quinn sat down. He knew if he didn't push his friend along that she would never go on a second date with him.

"No, he's going to call me later on today." Quinn's heart skipped a beat at the thought. *Honestly, I need to drop this man soon before I get in too deep.*

"Okay good. That's a very promising sign. Shows he's interested. Very interested." François was hopeful.

"Stop it!"

"Stop what?" He asked innocently.

"Stop this! Stop this…this…*thing*, you're doing."

"What *thing* am I doing?" François feigned confusion.

"You know very well what. You're never happy, you're always pushing for more." Quinn gave her friend a knowing smirk.

"You think you know me so well." François acted hurt.

"Don't you pull that on me. You know very well I'm right."

Relenting, François said, "Okay fine, but you know as well as I do that he's the guy for you. You just won't admit it."

"There is no 'guy' for me as you so eloquently stated."

"Oh yes there is and his name is Darcy! Well, at the very least you need to go on that second date with him, so when is it going to happen?"

"We've had our second date." Quinn tried to divert her friend.

"Oh no you haven't and don't try to get out of it. That's our deal. You go on a second date and if you still aren't interested then I'll leave you be."

"Well, I don't even know if, or when, our second date might be because he's away on business this week."

"Okay, Q, but I'm keeping tabs on you. I'm not letting you off the hook. It's time for you to move on from Spencer."

Having had quite enough, Quinn stuck her tongue out at her friend.

"Nice." he responded, shaking his head in disbelief. "Mature."

Just then her phone rang and Quinn quickly picked it up, grateful to have the opportunity to escape the third degree François was giving her.

Knowing his friend would be happy to escape their conversation, François picked up his drink and took a sip. Looking over to the entrance of the cafe François waved as he saw someone familiar come in. The place was bustling today with a long line up of customers waiting to place their orders and several waiting for their completed drink orders before heading back out to the cold. Glancing over to the counter François noticed that Jorge was working today. Jorge was Dills and Dolls longest serving employee and no one could put together drinks more efficiently than Jorge who was at this very moment focused on filling those orders as quickly as possible.

The noise of the cafe was actually quite comforting to François. He liked that feeling of warmth emanating from the fireplace located in the middle of the room on this cool day. The hustle and bustle of staff filling drink orders, the Espresso machine hissing as it worked, the clanging of cutlery and dishes, the laughter and excited conversation taking place at the different tables around them, people working away on their laptops. This was his sanity…this is why he came here.

Turning his attention back to Quinn, François was curious who called.

"I had a good time too, Darcy." Quinn couldn't help but smile. Looking up at François, who became instantly interested in the conversation, Quinn rolled her eyes as she watched him put his hands to his heart mocking her.

"I'm busy preparing for an important presentation this week but I thought I would give you a call to see if you would be interested in going to dinner on the weekend?"

"Well, I would love to except I'm going to visit my grandmother on Friday for a few days."

"Okay, well, how about we get together when you return?" Darcy asked.

"Um…sure…I guess we can do that." Once again, looking up at François she frowned seeing him blowing her kisses. Even though he was kidding around she could tell he was scrutinizing her call.

"Call me when you get home and we'll make plans then. I can't talk long because I have another meeting to get to but is François there with you?"

"Yes, François is right here."

"Can I speak with him?"

"Oh, okay sure, just one second." Confused, Quinn handed François her phone and said, "Darcy would like to speak with you."

"Really?" François was intrigued.

"Hi Darcy. What's up?" This was followed up by 'Yes, of course.', 'Yes, perfect', 'Not a problem', yes, my mobile is 495-555-9296, then "I'll give you back to Quinn. Nice talking to you."

Handing Quinn back her phone, François got up and went to the counter to order another latte.

"Hi Darcy. What was that about?"

"Ah, but if I told you I would have to kill you," he teased.

Quinn laughed. She didn't want to admit it but her curiosity was piqued.

"Well, I better get going, I'm being summoned into the meeting now. Enjoy the visit with your grandmother and I'll talk to you when you get home."

"I will, thanks."

"Oh, and Quinn?"

"Yes?"

"I can't wait to see you again."

Darcy was quite genuine when he spoke and it made Quinn feel uncomfortable. She wasn't used to someone being so sincere with her and she wasn't quite sure how to respond.

"Oh…yeah, sure. Talk to you…" She felt completely self-conscious and she hated it.

Hanging up the phone, she had mixed emotions. On one hand she felt flattered that Darcy seemed to care about her and couldn't wait to see her again. Yet on the other hand she felt anxious because he was chipping away at the armour protecting her heart and that just wasn't something she was ready for. Not yet. Maybe not ever.

Having left François at Dills and Dolls, Quinn arrived home and thought about starting to pack for her grandmother's. She was going to leave Friday but wanted to get an early start.

Hearing a knock at her door, Quinn ran to open it and to her surprise it was a delivery person.

"Are you Quinn Fairchild?" He mundanely asked.

"Yes, I am."

"These are for you, then." And with that he quickly handed her the long package, turned and headed for the elevator.

Shutting her door, Quinn walked into the kitchen, placed the box on the counter, opened it up and was speechless to see a dozen red roses with baby's breath inside. Noticing a card, she picked it up and reading it, tears came to her eyes.

> *Quinn*
>
> *I had a great time the other night and look forward to many more great times together.*
>
> *Love Darcy*

Quinn couldn't believe he sent flowers to her. No one had ever sent her a dozen red roses before. *This man sure knows how to 'hit a home run' straight to my heart. Damn him!*

Placing the flowers in a vase, Quinn picked up the phone and called François.

"What do you mean, you know? How could you know Darcy sent me flowers?"

"Because when I spoke to him earlier, he asked me if you would like having flowers sent to you, specifically red roses. Can I tell you, if you're stupid enough to let this man go then I'm going to snatch him up myself because he's some kinda man! He's got looks, personality, a breathtaking physique and on top of all of that, he's a romantic! Don't ruin this, Q!"

Laughing, Quinn said, "Yeah, yeah, yeah. You're so easily charmed, François."

"Yes, well, and you should be too. Not everyone is as lucky, so you better not waste it. Anyway, must go, Fayeed is yelling down the hall at me. No doubt, some crisis in his own mind. Talk when you get back from your grandmother's."

Hanging up with her friend, Quinn looked over at the flowers sitting prominently on her fireplace mantle and enjoyed the feeling of knowing someone cared about her.

FIFTEEN

*T*hursday morning arrived and Quinn awoke to her phone ringing and ignored it. She was tired and didn't want to answer it and promptly fell back to sleep again. After she heard it ringing for the third time, she finally decided to pick it up.

"Hello?" she answered sleepily.

"Quinn, it's your mother."

Dammit what does she want now?

"Yes mother, what do you want?" Quinn asked defensively.

"Quinn, I need you to come home immediately." Quinn noticed her mother's voice sounded uncharacteristically emotional.

"Why do I need to come home, Mother? I thought we said all we needed to say the other day to each other."

"Quinn, your grandmother died last night."

Quinn's heart seemed to stop and she had trouble breathing while tears immediately welled up in her eyes.

"What?!" She could barely get the word out. It took all of her strength to keep from falling apart. "What do you mean Grandma died? I was just speaking with her on Monday. She sounded fine. What happened?" Quinn was beginning to shake.

"She apparently died in her sleep. Old age I suppose. Not a surprise, she was ancient. That handyman down the street who is constantly mooching from her said he found her when she didn't come to the door. He had apparently come to do yet more work for her. I personally feel he targeted her as easy money…"

Quinn could barely focus on what her mother was saying. She was in shock about her grandmother. *How could this be? I was just speaking with her. She can't be dead.*

"…so, we are going to have a memorial for her right away…get this business done and over with…will need to speak with her lawyer about her will…"

Quinn's thoughts were racing. *This can't be true. I'm going to visit her tomorrow. She seemed fine when I spoke to her.*

"…catered. I'm sure there won't be many there. God, I hate funerals. They are so depressing."

Suddenly acknowledging what her mother was saying, Quinn grew angry.

"What are you talking about, Mother? Grandma is dead. How could you be so selfish?"

"It's got nothing to do with being selfish, Quinn, it has everything to do with the fact that the timing of her death is very inconvenient. Your father and I were supposed to be in the city this week for a very important meeting. Besides, this dying business is all just a big cash grab. The government manages to tax everything, including death."

"Oh my God, Mother!" Quinn couldn't believe what she was hearing. Well, she could believe it, in fact.

"Oh Quinn, for God's sake, relax! You're so sensitive. You always take things to heart. I expect you to come home right away. We are going to have the memorial as soon as possible. Get it done and over with. I'm sure no one will come except us. She was so old, I'm sure all of her friends are dead and gone by now."

"You are unbelievably heartless! You're not upset that Grandma has died. You're upset that it's screwing up your plans." Quinn was infuriated.

"Of course I'm upset about your grandmother dying, Quinn! What a terrible thing to say to me right now."

"It certainly doesn't sound that way. It's all about the inconvenience for God's sake!" Quinn was incensed by her mother's lack of compassion.

"That's completely unfair and I won't put up with this from you, Quinn." There was a moment of silence before her mother spoke again. "Now, when will you be home?"

"I'll be there tomorrow morning."

Quinn hung the phone up quickly and immediately began sobbing. *Oh Grandma, why did you have to leave me? We were going to have our girls' weekend together. What am I going to do without you?*

All she wanted to do was call François and although she knew he would come immediately, she also knew he was in the middle of a crisis at work and she didn't want to bother him. Lying on her bed, Quinn cried for what seemed like hours, eventually falling asleep.

Waking up, she looked at the time and seeing that it was after dinner, called François.

"Oh my God, Q, I'll be right over with a bottle of wine." Hesitating, he added, "Well, perhaps two bottles."

Within the hour, Quinn heard a knock on the door and in walked her friend, bottles of wine in hand. Rushing in, he placed the wine on the counter and immediately hugged Quinn who sobbed on his shoulder.

Eventually, calming down enough to speak, Quinn grabbed some tissue and loudly blew her nose.

"I don't know what I'm going to do without her, François. Beside you, she was my champion, the only other sane person in my family. How in God's name am I going to deal with the crazies on my own? My God, my mother was commenting about how 'inconvenient' it was that my grandmother died this week because they had a fucking meeting to go to! What the hell is wrong with those people?"

"That's ridiculous!" François was disheartened at what he was hearing, although not surprised.

Pulling out a couple of wine glasses, François opened the wine and poured them each a glass.

"Truth be told though, Quinn, they've always been like that and you know it. This is nothing new. I have no idea how you ended up so... well...normal."

Sitting quietly thinking, Quinn felt numb.

"I just can't believe she's gone, François."

"Q, I'm devastated for you, Sweetheart. I loved your grandmother. She was such a wonderful lady. I'll never forget the day she told me how she and your grandfather had been protesting some government bill that would have allowed the forest near their cabin be bulldozed over so they, and the crowd, ended up being watered down by some giant fire hose and they had to walk home soaking wet in the middle of the night. They were in their seventies at that time for God's sake! Your grandparents always amazed me. Thank God that bill never passed or I'm sure the local government would have had to answer to your grandparents and it wouldn't have been pretty. They were great people."

François' heart broke for his friend. He, himself, was upset by the loss of Esther so he couldn't imagine how devastated Quinn was feeling right now.

Quinn's eyes were swollen and red from crying, she looked exhausted.

"When is her funeral?" François asked.

"No funeral, just a memorial. Apparently, they will need to speak to my grandmother's lawyer..." Quinn absently stared into her glass of wine.

"Why didn't your grandmother use your father as her lawyer?" François was curious.

"They didn't want my parents involved in their business. She and my grandfather decided a long time ago to have their own lawyer. They never really liked my father. Hell, they barely tolerated my mother and vice versa, although they loved my parents, and my parents them, they just didn't understand each other."

Pouring Quinn more wine, François ordered pizza.

"I'm here for the night, Q, if you need me." François was not about to leave his friend in this emotional state.

"Thanks, François. How are things going with finding a replacement for Monica?"

"Don't even ask. Fayeed is completely fucking this whole thing up and I'm staying out of it. I will not be responsible for any of it."

"Well, I'm sure you'll find someone to fill in."

"Not before I lose my mind." François poured himself another glass of wine.

The evening was quiet. François and Quinn ate pizza, drank wine and watched TV, which Quinn mindlessly watched.

By midnight she insisted that François go home and get some sleep. She knew his days were busy and she didn't want her friend to worry about her. After he left, Quinn crawled into bed, under the blankets, fully dressed and cried herself to sleep once more.

SIXTEEN

*T*he next morning Quinn arrived at her parents' home in Upper Springdale, a gated estate community where no lot was smaller than five acres. She was greeted at the door by her mother instructing her that they were immediately leaving for the lawyer's office.

"Why now? Do we really need to have an appointment with him now?"

"Yes, Quinn, we must go now. Mr. Foster is going away on holiday tomorrow morning and needs to take care of business prior to his departure. I told you, your grandmother's death comes at a very inconvenient time."

Her mother was impeccably dressed in a black dress complete with black gloves and pill hat with a short veil reaching just below her nose. *A tad extreme but that's mother for you. Grandma would have said it was all for show.* Quinn had to agree.

As she stood there, not particularly shocked by her mother's lack of compassion, Quinn's father, sister and her fiancé, Bradley, all walked past her through the door.

"Hello Quinn." Her father offered curtly.

"Quinn, nice of you to show up." Her sister's sarcasm didn't go unnoticed.

"Quinn." Bradley sheepishly nodded as he passed by.

What a pathetic bunch, Quinn shook her head.

• ● •

Arriving at Mr. Foster's office, the entire family took their seats in the board room. Once Mr. Foster arrived, he sat down at the head of the table and opened his file. He looked much like what Quinn envisioned a grandfather would look like. Grey hair, glasses, warm, friendly face.

"Good morning. Thank you for meeting me on such short notice and at such a difficult time. As you may, or may not be aware, Esther had some definite ideas of how she wanted to disperse her estate and I am here today to present the reading of her will. I will be sure to present a copy to each of you before leaving today."

Clearing his throat, Mr. Foster began detailing how the general disbursements of Esther's estate would be distributed to her parents and sister with no mention of Quinn. Mr. Foster then took a moment to sip on the glass of water that sat in front of him.

Seizing the opportunity, Madison decided to offer her 'two-cents worth'.

"Well, clearly Grandmother had enough of your ridiculous lifestyle or she would have left you something." Madison smirked unsympathetically.

Quinn had to admit she was a little hurt that her grandmother hadn't left her anything but she really didn't care, she had her memories and she knew her grandmother loved her. No amount of 'stuff' or money could bring her back or take away all the wonderful memories she had of the time they had spent together.

"Even that hideous cabin can be sold now, isn't that right, Mother?"

Hearing what Madison said, Quinn quickly looked up at her sister realizing that she had been so caught up in the proceedings she, just then, realized that the cabin hadn't been mentioned at all, however, before she could say anything Mr. Foster quickly interjected.

"Oh, I'm not yet finished, Miss Fairchild."

Quinn quickly moved her gaze over to Mr. Foster as he addressed her sister, who immediately lost the smirk off her face.

Looking back down at the papers in front of him Mr. Foster continued.

"And now, in the matter of the property located on Morgan Lake in Morgansview at 13692 Brownie Lane, Esther's current residence. Excluding items previously indicated, the said land, cabin and everything on said property including *everything…*"

Quinn found it strange the word 'everything' was so clearly emphasized.

"…within the cabin is to fully, completely and without question, go to Quinn Esther Fairchild."

"What?!" Quinn's mother, father and sister all echoed their shock. Bradley knew well enough to keep his mouth shut.

Quinn's mouth dropped open. "What?! All of it to *me?*" She was as surprised as the rest of the family. "Are you sure?" She wanted confirmation.

"Yes, I'm quite sure, Miss Fairchild." Mr. Foster was confident with his response.

"Well that seems rather unfair to my other daughter, Madison, Mr. Foster." Thomas expressed his indignation.

"As you are fully aware, Mr. Fairchild, in our business, family wills are not necessarily based on fairness."

Mr. Foster was quite aware of the family dynamics. Esther had filled him in a long time ago and he knew that Esther's relationship with her grand-daughter, Quinn, was of great importance to her. He was also very much aware that the others had no interest in spending time with Esther, let alone any interest in her cabin.

"But Mr. Foster, my mother surely would have left something more for Madison. I can't believe for one moment that the majority of her estate would go to Quinn…"

"Mother!" Quinn was shocked at her mother's obvious shallow disregard for her feelings.

"Well, it doesn't seem right, Quinn. Your grandmother and Madison were very close. I would almost suggest they were closer than…"

"Mrs. Fairchild." Mr. Foster quickly interjected, "Once again, wills are not about dispersing estates fairly, they are entirely about dispersing estates according to the wishes of the deceased. This is a fully verified will as I wrote it up for your mother myself. If you have any thought of contesting it, let me assure you that you would not win." Mr. Foster was firm.

Quinn looked at her family and realized just how pathetic and selfish they truly were. They couldn't even allow her this last gift from her grandmother without a scene. Quinn sat quietly and let Mr. Foster fight the battle with her family.

Finishing up, Mr. Foster looked around the room. "Are there any other questions that I can answer?"

Noticing the obvious eye-rolling and sighing that took place, Mr. Foster was pleased that this family knew enough to keep their mouths shut at that particular moment.

"No? Right then, here is a copy for all of you and the papers I require signed. I will be sure to distribute the funds to each of you as quickly as possible. Quinn if you could stay for just a moment. I have some separate papers for you to sign. I would like to thank all of you for coming in so quickly and if I could have a few moments with Quinn privately, I won't keep her long as I'm sure you would like to get home." Mr. Foster waited until they all left the room, grumbling to themselves as they went, before addressing Quinn.

"Now Quinn, do you fully understand what your grandmother has left you? It is all of her land on Morgan Lake which amounts to approximately twenty-five acres, the cabin that she has been living in, her pick up truck and the big shed on the property. She wanted me to be perfectly clear with you that *everything in* and out of the cabin and on the property, belongs to you and only you, other than the few items in the cabin previously mentioned that Esther willed to the rest of your family, of course. Do you understand this?"

"Um, yes, I understand that Mr. Foster, thank you." Quinn was confused as to why he felt the need to so dramatically emphasize this point with her.

"Okay, then, I have some papers for you to sign, which will give you full ownership of the property, truck, etc. The property is mortgage free, of course. Your grandfather had it all paid off before he died." Sliding papers across his table towards Quinn, together with a pen, he waited patiently while she read the documentation over and then signed all the papers where he had indicated. Once completed, Mr. Foster provided a copy of everything to Quinn, along with the ownership and keys.

"Your grandmother was very organized and had all of this sorted out quite some time ago. Now, this does require processing and my office will take care of it as quickly as possible but trust me, as of right now, you are the sole and legal owner of that property and can come and go as you please."

"Thank you, Mr. Foster. I appreciate all that you have done for my grandmother." Quinn felt quite emotional.

"My pleasure, and Quinn…"

Quinn looked up at Mr. Foster.

"I think you should know that your grandmother spoke very highly of you. She loved you very much. She always said you had a good head on your shoulders."

Nodding, Quinn was too choked up to speak. It meant a lot to hear what Mr. Foster had to say…more than he would ever know.

Pausing momentarily, he continued, "I liked your grandmother very much; she was a remarkable lady. I will miss her a great deal."

Mr. Foster stood up and reached his hand out to shake Quinn's. Shaking it, Quinn couldn't even begin to imagine that she now owned her grandparents' cabin. The one that she herself loved so much.

"Good luck, Quinn. Should you require any further assistance please feel free to contact me at any time. It was a pleasure to serve your grandmother for the many years I did and it would be a pleasure to offer my services to you as well."

Wiping away tears, Quinn's mind was racing. She needed time to sort through her thoughts and everything that had just taken place.

"Thank you, Mr. Foster. I appreciate that very much and I'm sure you will be hearing from me in the not too distant future." Walking out of Mr. Foster's office Quinn was still trying to absorb everything Mr. Foster relayed to her. Looking up at her family, she realized this was no time for conversation and kept walking out the front door. The ride home was quiet and uncomfortable. It had begun to rain while they had been in Mr. Foster's office and Quinn sat quietly listening to the rain splattering on the windshield and the sound of the windshield wipers swishing back and forth.

Back at her parents' home, she hadn't expected the deluge of opinions she would receive from the entire family...well, she expected it but thought they would at least have waited until after her grandmother was buried.

"I personally think you should sell that old shack. It's falling apart anyway." Madison eagerly offered.

"Quinn, I would agree with Madison. I have no idea what your grandmother saw in that place. There is nothing appealing about it at all. You should definitely sell it." Quinn's mother was more than happy to agree with Madison.

"The real estate market is good right now, Quinn. It's the perfect time to sell. I know an excellent agent, Marshall Fox, best realtor in the area. I'll give him a call in the morning for you and set up an appointment." Her father seemed far too eager to push the sale of the property along.

Again, Bradley knew enough to keep his opinions to himself for fear of repercussion from anyone.

Sitting quietly listening to her family ramble on, Quinn finally spoke.

"No. I'll not be selling it." Quinn wanted to be quite clear about her intentions.

"What?! You do realize that it's not worth the land it was built on, for God's sake, Quinn." her father was emphatic.

"I'm not selling." Quinn was determined not to let them push her around.

"Don't be ridiculous, Quinn. You *must* sell it, surely you see that. I'm sure your grandmother would be very happy to have you sell and get the money, considering you are unemployed," her mother insisted.

Quinn refused to respond.

By the time lunch was over, Quinn had just about enough of her family. Her emotions were raw and she grew tired of being told… actually, goaded, to sell and finally lost what little patience she had left.

"Enough! That's it! You know what? I can't take this anymore. I'm leaving. You people have done nothing but push me to sell since we got home from Mr. Foster's office and Grandma isn't even buried yet. You all know very well how much that place meant to her and…well…to me, too! I have no intention of selling. I'm going home and when you have a date set for the memorial let me know." She headed for the front door to grab her coat and purse.

Her father grew angry with his eldest daughter.

"Quinn, don't be so preposterous! You must listen to reason. You have no idea what you are getting yourself into. You can't even take care of yourself for heaven's sake, how do you expect to deal with twenty-five acres of property and a cabin with no money, no job prospects and well, quite frankly, no husband?"

Quinn knew this was purely rhetorical and as furious as she was, she had no energy to respond to her father's total disrespect for her, anyway. Opening the front door, Quinn said nothing.

"There won't be a memorial." Her mother yelled after her.

Stopping and turning around, Quinn asked, "Why not?"

Looking uncomfortable, her mother continued. "She didn't want one, apparently. She wanted to be…" Quinn's mother rolled her eyes and sighed with annoyance. "She wanted to be cremated for God's sake and if you can bloody well believe it…" Hesitating she finally added, "…have her ashes spread all over that dreadful property of hers."

"I thought you said she wanted a memorial. Mr. Foster said nothing about this when we met today."

"Yes, well, he informed us this morning that her wishes were otherwise. What an absolutely disgusting thought but I suppose we will have to abide by her wishes, according to that annoying Mr. Foster. Your grandmother always was…" thinking carefully, she added, "….different."

Quinn couldn't take it anymore. "You know what, Mother? You're a pretentious bitc…" Gathering her thoughts for a moment, Quinn continued, "How about we not have any contact for a while and you can let me know when her ashes are ready and I'll let you know when you can come to *my* property to spread them and retrieve what items she did will to you. And if it is too disgusting for you, then you can stay away and I'll damn well spread them myself." Quinn was fed up. Walking out the door her mother called out to her.

"Quinn, you had better be careful or you will lose your family to that haughty attitude of yours."

Quinn shouted, "Before you accuse me of having a haughty attitude, Mother, perhaps you all should have a good long look in the mirror." Slamming the door behind her, Quinn wanted to cry but fought back any tears. She felt empowered for the first time in a very long time.

Take that and stick it where the sun doesn't shine!

Taking a step out onto the walkway, Quinn immediately slipped and fell, landing hard on her butt.

"Ow! Dammit! You would think they could have their walkway cleared of wet leaves considering the amount of money they pay Thomas to maintain their property." Tears came to her eyes as she struggled to stabilize her footing and stand up but slipped and fell once again. Not even trying to get up this time she just sat on the wet ground. It took only a moment for her to begin sobbing.

Giving herself a few minutes to regain her composure, the sobbing slowed up and she wiped away the tears and runny nose with her scarf, sniffling as she did. Turning onto her hands and knees she pushed herself up to a standing position and grew angry.

Reaching her car, she got in and slammed the door shut. She was cold, wet and now full of pent up anger. All she wanted to do was go home. Starting to cry again, she was frustrated by the events of the day.

"You know what, Grandma? You're going to get your wish. You can count on it," she said aloud as she sniffled and once again wiped her nose with her scarf before starting the long drive home. *I really must learn to carry tissue.*

SEVENTEEN

*H*aving cried much of the way home, Quinn was exhausted and although it was early evening she felt ready for bed. Unlocking the door to her condo she breathed a sigh of relief as she shut the door behind her and hung up her coat.

"Home sweet home and some sanity."

Changing out of her wet clothes and into her pajamas, Quinn headed to the kitchen to grab a glass of wine and a snack. Looking in her fridge, she realized that because she was supposed to be going to her grandmother's the next day, she had few groceries.

"I guess I had better call Darcy and let him know I'll be home now." Although she was confused by her relationship with him, she felt the need to see things through and told herself that it was all in the name of appeasing her friend who clearly had no intention of letting her off the hook.

Dialling his mobile phone, Quinn waited for him to answer but was shocked when a woman's voice echoed across the line.

"Hello?" The woman's voice answered amongst a lot of commotion in the background.

Quinn didn't say anything at first. *I must have dialled the wrong number.*

"Hello? Who is this?" The woman asked.

The voice sounded vaguely familiar but Quinn couldn't place it. She was having difficulty hearing because of the noise in the background so she was sure the woman who answered would be as well so she spoke a little louder than normal.

"Um, hello? I must have the wrong number. I'm looking for Darcy, Darcy Monaghan."

"I'm sorry…quite loud…breaking in and out…can't hear…looking for Darcy?"

"Yes, I am, but I must have the wrong number."

"This is Darcy's phone."

"Oh, okay. Well, could you tell him Quinn is calling?" Quinn had to admit the connection at the other end was terrible.

"Who? I'm sorry…difficult to hear."

"It's Quinn calling." Quinn shouted into the phone.

"Lynn?"

"No," she was annoyed. *Damn this is a lousy connection.*

"Unfortunately, Darcy is on stage…twenty minutes… giving a speech with… his wife."

Quinn couldn't think straight. *Wife? Did she hear that correctly?* Her insecurities immediately kicked in.

"Hello? Hello? Can I have him call… off stage?" Quinn could hear the other woman speaking to someone else. "Damn this connection… can't hear…"

Quinn immediately hung up the phone. It was more than she could take right now. She was emotionally falling apart. Her heart felt like it was about to explode.

"Wife? That bastard has a wife? I knew I couldn't trust him! He's just like Spencer!" The tears began flowing down her cheeks. Throwing herself down onto the couch she sobbed uncontrollably. She felt like her life was completely falling apart around her. Nothing was going right.

Within the hour her home phone began to ring. Looking at the display she saw that it was Darcy. She pulled the plug out of the wall. She didn't even want to listen to it knowing it was him at the other end.

Moments later, her mobile was ringing. Darcy again. Turning the volume off she then threw it across the room. Quinn's tears had stopped, anger had taken over.

"It's over, Darcy Monaghan. Does your wife even know you've been cheating on her? No, I'm sure she wouldn't. How could I have been such a fool? I let my guard down and this is what happens. Well, no more. I'm done with you and I'm done with men for a very long time."

After crying for what seemed like hours, Quinn was exhausted. It had been the day from hell and she was completely drained emotionally. Thinking back to her grandmother the sadness was all encompassing.

"Aw, Grandma…how am I ever going to manage without you? I miss you so much already. Nothing is going right." Tears came to her eyes again and Quinn gave up on the idea of a snack, sat down in front of her gas fireplace and quietly sipped on wine in the dark.

Before she knew it, she had fallen asleep only to awake almost two hours later. Still feeling completely exhausted, she glanced over to where she had thrown her phone. Picking it up, she looked at it. Darcy had tried to call her more than a dozen times. François also had tried to call once. She wasn't in the mood to speak to anyone. The many messages left, she deleted without listening to them.

"Fuck you, Darcy Monaghan," she said groggily.

Turning off her fireplace, Quinn headed to bed. She was angry with herself for allowing her defences to lower with Darcy. She should have known better. On top of everything else, she dreaded going to the cabin. It was going to be another emotional shot to the heart and she wasn't sure she could survive it.

Plopping herself face down on top of her bed, she grabbed her pillow, shoved it under her head almost hugging it. All she was sure about was, that she didn't have the energy to figure anything out tonight and with that, she once again cried herself to sleep.

EIGHTEEN

The next morning she awoke to an overcast, rainy day. Closing her eyes again, she moaned, rolled over onto her back and lay there staring at the ceiling listening to the rain fall. *Hard to believe it's the beginning of November,* she thought.

She was emotionally drained and physically stiff all over as if she had slept in the same position all night long but most likely because of her fall. Looking at the clock, she was shocked to see that it was almost noon. Walking out to the kitchen she plugged her home phone back in again and couldn't help but notice a light flashing on her answering machine indicating she had messages. She felt better prepared this morning to deal with Darcy. Anger had taken over from the hurt and as far as she was concerned she was better off without that cheating bastard in her life.

Hitting the button, she was prepared for all of the messages to be from Darcy but was relieved she was wrong.

"Q, it's me François. Darcy called looking for you. Call the man back for chrissakes! I know you've been busy with your family so I didn't want to bother you. How did things go with them or do I even need to ask? By the way, I'm living my own nightmare here. Fayeed's idea of a good candidate was some model that looked like she just finished a night out on the streets, so you can well imagine what I had to say about that. It's a good thing we are friends is all I have to say. God knows this is going to be a very long, trying proce…"

Quinn found herself smiling because François often left messages that were way too long for her machine. She hit the button to listen to the next message.

"Q, it's me, again. When will you get an answering machine that will last longer than thirty seconds for recording messages? You know I can't leave a message in that short of a time. By the time I start the damn message, I'm being cut off because there is no more time left. It drives me absolutely fucking crazy. You know very well I hate that bloody machine of yours. It's a piece of shit! Sometimes, I think you keep it just to irritate me. No, I'm sure you do! Anyway, what I was actually calling you abou…"

Although she was in a terrible mood, Quinn couldn't help but chuckle and hit the button once again.

"Oh my fucking God! I fucking hate that fucking machine of yours!"

This time she laughed out loud. Yelling into the machine François finally conceded, gave a heavy sigh of defeat, and said, "Just call me."

Hitting the button once again, the smile was wiped off her face instantly.

"Quinn, it's Darcy. Hey, listen, François told me about your grandmother. I'm sorry to hear she passed away. Call me."

"Fuck you!"

She assumed the next couple of messages were the same although she wouldn't know because she deleted them as soon as she heard his voice.

"I'm done with you. No second chances." She felt the need to speak out loud almost as if doing so would solidify her decision.

Hitting the button for the final message, she wasn't any happier listening to it.

"Quinn, it's your father. How dare you speak to your mother the way you did last evening. She was extremely upset after you left. I mean, after all, she just lost her mother and you were completely disrespectful, not to mention irrational, with absolutely no regard for her feelings. I expect you to call her back and offer an apology."

106

"Yeah, right. I can assure you that isn't going to happen."

Quinn just couldn't shake the dark frame of mind she was in. Everything was a mess, nothing seemed to be going right since her grandmother died.

After forcing herself to eat something, Quinn decided to put Darcy out of her mind and look over the papers Mr. Foster had given her. She grew sad at the sight of her grandmother's keys to the cabin and the pick-up truck. They were on an old key ring her grandfather had made for her grandmother's birthday many years ago and it was a key ring her grandmother had never been willing to change. It was made out of cedar wood from their property and her grandfather had carved it into the shape of a heart with both their initials carved on the one side of it. On the back he had very crudely hand carved the date 4/30/88, the date they took possession of the cabin. Quinn smiled at the thought of such a loving gesture. Her grandparents had a love for each other that Quinn could only hope for but now realized that she would likely never find.

"Well, Grandma, I know I should go to the cabin but I can't even think about going right now...not without you..." Tears began to flow once again. Shaking it off, Quinn got dressed then called François to update him on the turn of events.

"Hello, François here."

"François, it's Quinn."

"Oh, hey Quinn, are you calling to tell me you threw that fucking answering machine out the window?"

"No, I am not because I did not."

"Are you calling me to say that you finally called Darcy back? He called me wondering what was going on so I did tell him about your grandmother."

"No I didn't call Darcy back and I'll get to that in a minute. You'll never guess what happened last night. It's been a complete fucking nightmare." Going into detail about her visit to the lawyer's office and then the argument with her mother afterwards, Quinn explained how her father wanted her to apologize. She finally wrapped up the conversation with what had taken place with Darcy.

"First of all, no, that can't be true about Darcy. I don't believe it." François had his doubts that his friend's theory was right.

"Well, it is true, I heard it with my own ears. What a cheating bastard he is."

Thinking for a few moments, François offered, "Are you sure you heard correctly? I mean, you did say that it was a very broken connection. Maybe she wasn't talking about him."

"Who else would she be talking about? I mean, I was calling for Darcy why would she be talking about someone else's wife? I think it was pretty damn clear."

"Well, I suppose…just make sure you're right, Q. Darcy just didn't give me the vibe that he is a cheating bastard kind of guy." François wasn't convinced his friend was correct. He knew she was skittish when it came to men and looked for any reason to kick them to the curb and he was thinking this might be one of those times. *I think I'll give Darcy a call back and find out for myself. I've still got his number from when I ordered those flowers for him. If she's wrong, she deserves to know and if she's right, he needs his ass kicked.*

"I don't want to talk about him anymore. I'm sick of the whole thing." She was hurt, angry and felt completely humiliated.

"I'm thinking of going to my grandmother's…" Pausing for a moment, Quinn continued, "…*my* cabin for a couple of weeks. I'm dreading it but I know I should go."

"So, to be perfectly clear, does this mean that you now own the cabin? All twenty-five acres of it?" François was a bit overwhelmed by everything he had heard and was having a hard time getting past the Darcy part of their conversation, let alone hearing that Quinn now owned the cabin and all the land.

"Yeah." She answered slowly. "I guess it does."

"Q, that's amazing! Better you than anyone else in your family." *God knows I wouldn't want to stay out in the middle of nowhere but I know how much Q loves that place.*

"Yes, but naturally it was all unfair to Madison. It's not a surprise that my parents and sister are all telling me to sell. I can't do it François. My grandparents loved that place, not to mention, I love it. My grandfather redecorated the place almost completely when they first bought it. There are so many great memories there. How can I give that up?" She was looking for affirmation from her friend that she was right in her decision to keep it.

"Listen Q. If you aren't sure that you are making the right decision then go to the cabin for the couple of weeks and see how you feel there. If it feels right then keep it. If it doesn't, then perhaps selling it is the best option but you won't know until you go back. I mean, there's no hurry, even if you did want to sell. Take your time, it doesn't matter if it takes weeks, months or even years before you know what you want to do. Think on it before making any decisions. Don't let your family pressure you."

"But it's going to be so hard to go there without her, François." Tears quickly came to her eyes.

"Well, you should at least just go check on the place. I mean, it's getting colder. You may want to be sure that…I don't know…that the heat is on or something…" François wasn't sure how to help his friend and being practical wasn't one of his strong suits but it seemed like the right advice to offer at the moment. His heart broke for her. "It'll give you time to think."

She was contemplating what François said when he broke the silence asking, "Are you going to tell Darcy about the cabin?"

"What? No! I don't have the strength to get into anything with him right now, or ever for that matter, so maybe going to the cabin for a couple of weeks isn't such a bad idea. Everything is just so overwhelming."

Thinking for a moment she offered, "Besides, we're done now anyway. Remember? He's a cheating bastard."

"Well, I still think you may be wrong." François wasn't convinced about that telephone call.

"Listen, must go. Fayeed has arranged for another interview shortly and they sure as hell better wow me this time and not look like the local hooker. Call me when you get back home. Stay strong. Love you, Q. Call Darcy."

"I told you, I'm not going to call…" Hearing François hang up the phone, Quinn put the receiver down and contemplated what her friend had said. Quinn reluctantly agreed with him about the cabin, but not Darcy. "I suppose he's right. I really don't want to go but I suppose I do need to check on the place. I'm not sure what state it's in but I sure as hell am not going to call that cheating bastard."

Taking most of the day to pack her two suitcases Quinn decided to procrastinate a little longer and leave first thing in the morning. Relieved that Darcy finally quit calling her, she went to bed early and quickly fell into a deep sleep.

NINETEEN

*T*he next day, Quinn laid in bed dreading the thought of leaving for the cabin. The last thing she wanted was to be at the cabin alone but knew she needed to get used to it if she was going to keep the place. Besides, she needed to get away. Between Darcy and her family, she needed to escape.

Loading up her car, she headed out. She was nervous knowing that her grandmother wouldn't be there but the more she thought about it, the more she felt obligated to go. She really did need to be sure everything was secure. It was the responsible thing to do.

It was a five-hour drive. She had planned to arrive long before dark and given how far out of town her grandmother lived, with not a person nor streetlight within miles, it made sense to get there early.

Arriving in Morgansview, Quinn pulled into the parking lot of the grocery store, picked up a few items she was sure she would need and headed back out of town towards the cabin.

Turning onto the unpaved driveway, Quinn became nostalgic remembering all the years she had spent there. It felt like she was coming back home.

It was a beautiful, sunny day. The air was cold and according to the cashier at the grocery store, they had been experiencing sporadic thunder storms recently. Mountain weather could be so unpredictable. As she drove up the long driveway, Quinn wound down the car window and took in a deep breath of the clean, cool, pine-scented air. She seemed to instantly relax and exhaling, she could see her breath in the air. Coming here was bittersweet.

Although the log cabin had been her grandparents' for almost thirty years, it was, in fact, more than a century old. She still couldn't believe it was willed to her and her alone. If she wasn't so heartbroken, she would have been elated. Regardless of what her parents and sister were demanding, she wasn't interested in selling. Quinn knew though, that reality would eventually set in and with no job prospects in sight, it would be impossible to keep the place given the debt she was already in.

Remembering the conversation with her grandmother on the phone just days ago, Quinn recalled how her grandmother had offered to give her money but, of course, she wouldn't hear of it. She would never have taken money from her grandmother. Although Quinn had reassured her grandmother that she was getting by on her severance, truth be told, she wasn't managing on the pittance of money she was receiving from her severance package or from unemployment.

Unfortunately, the cabin was showing signs of deterioration and Quinn knew it would be costly to fix up. The contractor her grandmother had apparently brought in a few years prior had said it was structurally sound but the costs associated with renovating would be astronomical. *Whatever astronomical means in dollars and cents*, Quinn thought.

Quinn was positive that, had her grandmother been able to afford to do the renovations, she would have done them by now. Quinn's dream of keeping it clearly didn't look hopeful. She just plain and simply didn't have the funds and she knew she may have to come to terms with that.

Pulling up in front, Quinn remained in her car and sat staring at the cabin. She had a knot in her stomach dreading this moment. Tears came to her eyes as she sat and remembered all the fun times here. She almost expected to see her grandmother come out the front door greeting her with open arms and a big smile on her face as always. She had a special relationship with her grandparents, she always had. After her grandfather died a couple of years ago, Quinn's bond with her grandmother strengthened more than ever. Her grandmother often said how Quinn was the only one in the family who truly understood and appreciated the respite the cabin offered from busy city life.

Opening the car door, Quinn stepped out onto the partially frozen ground. As she slammed the door shut, the sound resonated across the property. The trees were bare, allowing the sun to unreservedly shine through and she heard the haunting echo of a crow cawing in the distance. Her skin developed goose bumps as the cool air kissed her cheeks. Closing her eyes, listening to the breeze blowing through the trees, feeling the warmth of the sun on her face she briefly relaxed. The solitude was almost spiritual. Opening her eyes again, she grabbed her suitcases and placed them by the front door. Grabbing the few bags of groceries she had purchased she once again turned towards the cabin. She knew she could no longer delay the inevitable. Taking a slow deep breath in and then out again, she looked at the front door with reluctance. *Here goes.*

Unlocking the cabin door, she walked into a flood of familiar sights and smells that launched her back through decades of wonderful memories. Shutting the door behind her, she placed everything down and just stood there, the recognizable smell of pine and cedar comforting her as she scanned the cabin. Her eyes settled on her grandmother's hand-knit sweater coat and her heart skipped a beat. It was hanging in the front hall exactly where her grandmother would have left it, as if she had just worn it that morning.

Taking off her shoes and hanging up her own coat, Quinn headed into the living room and immediately walked over to her grandmother's old chair and sat down. All that could be heard was the methodical ticking of the clock mounted above the fireplace. The cabin was too quiet. Lonely. Empty. Devoid of its heart and soul. She was overwhelmed with sadness. Quinn leaned her head back onto the chair and closed her eyes, her mind almost blank. The tears began to flow freely.

Then a few moments later, almost as quickly as she started, Quinn stopped crying. She couldn't explain it but a strong sense of peace suddenly overcame her. She was alone and yet she somehow felt like her grandmother was right there with her, like she was speaking to her. *Life goes on, Quinn dear, but I will always be with you.*

Wiping away her tears with the palms of her hands, Quinn got up, grabbed the groceries from the hall and walked into the kitchen. Filling the kettle, she put it on the stove to boil for tea. It was always the first thing her grandmother did when Quinn came to visit. Unpacking the groceries into the cupboards, Quinn then emptied the fridge of any food that was no longer good and placed the fresh groceries on the near empty shelves. Shutting the fridge door, she turned around then leaned back against the small counter scanning the room. The kitchen was very rustic. Her grandfather had renovated it using nothing but materials from their own property. The cupboard doors were made from cedar trees and the floor of pine, all meticulously crafted by her grandfather. Her grandmother had often commented how much she loved this room. Glancing over, Quinn smiled as she saw her own initials carved into the floor near the kitchen table. Her parents had been so upset with her when they found out what she had done. She was only nine years old at the time and she smiled remembering her grandmother telling Quinn's mother, "Leave the child alone, Ruth. It's my floor and I personally love that I now have Quinn's initials etched into it for all time." *Grandma always came to my rescue.*

Opening one of the cupboards, Quinn chuckled discovering the many jars of peanut butter stashed away. Her grandmother loved peanut butter on toast for breakfast and always made sure she had plenty on hand. Reaching in, she was about to grab her grandmother's old tea tin and hesitated. Staring at it, she just couldn't bear to pull it out. Quinn instead decided to have the herbal tea she purchased from the grocery store, leaving the old tea tin in its place exactly where her grandmother had left it.

Sitting at the kitchen table, she blankly stared out the window in the direction of the woods. The sun was slowly working its way down the horizon and the shadows were getting longer. She didn't think about anything in particular. The cabin was uncomfortably quiet. Getting up, Quinn walked over to the counter and turned on her grandmother's old radio. She always wanted to give her grandmother a new, more up-to-date radio but her grandmother wouldn't hear of it. It had been a gift from her grandfather one Christmas and it still worked well, although in recent years it had become crackly sounding and harder to hear but it didn't matter to her grandmother. *I suppose it's my radio now. I can get any modern radio I want…but…I don't want. Somehow this old radio means so much more now. I couldn't give it up if I wanted to.*

Tears came to Quinn's eyes once more. *All I want to do is cry. I need to stop this.*

Hearing the tea kettle whistle, Quinn made herself a cup of tea and began going from room to room reminiscing. Walking back into the hall, Quinn grabbed her suitcases, went to the guest room and emptied the contents into the dresser. Picking up the empty suitcases she walked down the hall to put them into the front closet. As she did so, she walked past her grandmother's bedroom and stopped.

Staring into the room, Quinn's eyes filled with tears. Seeing the quilt on the bed, she smiled. *I remember Grandma making that quilt when I was a little girl.* Leaving the suitcases on the floor in the hall, Quinn made her way slowly into the bedroom, stopping to look around. The room still smelled very much of her grandmother's perfume. Seeing the picture of her grandparents on the night table didn't surprise her. It was always there, but it seemed even more poignant now than ever before. Walking towards the bed she leaned over and placed both hands, palms down, onto the quilt and closed her eyes, praying her grandmother would be there when she opened them again. The feel of the quilt brought back so many memories of her as a young girl taking naps on her grandmother's bed whenever she came to visit. She always loved lying there listening to her grandparents conversations with each other and laughing. It was safe. It always felt…comforting. Something she always felt when she was at the cabin.

Opening her eyes again, Quinn turned around and sat down on the edge of the bed. She looked up at all the pictures on the wall, mostly of her grandparents, some of Quinn and her sister, Madison, only a single photo of her parents. The room now felt so empty, cold. Sighing, Quinn laid down and placed her head on the pillow, taking a deep breath in. It too smelled like her grandmother. She pulled the quilt over her. It felt comforting, like she was enveloped by her grandmother. Closing her eyes, it wasn't long before she cried herself to sleep.

The next day Quinn awoke to a dull, overcast sky. *That figures. It feels the same way I do.* She didn't much feel like getting out of bed and it was only when she grew hungry that she made her way to the kitchen and made herself some toast and a coffee. Sitting at the kitchen table she stared miserably outside.

Quinn thought of her grandmother and how much she missed her. It was all like one big nightmare. *This can't really be happening. I'm sure any minute now Grandma is going to walk in here and tell me that breakfast is ready, that the blueberry pancakes and bacon were all mine because she was happy with her toast and peanut butter.* Quinn sighed. There wasn't the smell of pancakes and bacon cooking and her grandmother wasn't going to be walking into the kitchen. The heartache just wouldn't stop.

"Now what?" she asked herself. Closing her eyes she tried to envision her grandmother standing there. Opening them once again, she looked around the cold, empty kitchen with the single cup of tea still sitting on the counter where she had left it the night before and felt nothing but sadness.

"Aw the hell with it, I'm going back to bed."

Before crawling back into bed, Quinn realized she was still in the same clothes she had worn when she arrived and changed into some pajamas. Crawling back into her grandmother's bed she proceeded to sleep the day away, only getting up when she grew hungry or went to the washroom and then crawled back into bed once again. Turning in the direction of the window, Quinn stared out at the trees. *I don't want to sell this place, Grandma, but I don't have the money. I'm so sorry.* Tears streamed down her face. Shutting her eyes, Quinn once again cried herself to sleep.

Upon waking, it was dark outside and she was once again feeling hungry and decided to grab a bowl of cereal. It was pretty much all she could stomach right now. Sitting in the kitchen, Quinn stared mindlessly as she finished her food. Placing the bowl into the sink, she thought she should really do the dishes. They hadn't been done since she had arrived. *I'm tired. I'll do them later.*

Wandering down the hall, she turned a light on and noticed her suitcases still sitting where she had left them. Walking past them, she went and sat down in the living room and stared unemotionally into the cold, dark fireplace. Shivering, she reached for the blanket her grandmother always had sitting in a basket beside the chair and wrapped it around her. She couldn't even be bothered to turn on a light. The glow from the hall was sufficient. She had lost all track of time but didn't care.

After what seemed like hours, she tossed the blanket aside, stood up, then walked down the hall towards the bedroom. Not wanting to change, she crawled into bed. Sleep didn't come immediately because the cabin was so quiet. Too quiet. Usually her grandmother stayed up later than her, puttering away. Quinn had loved the routine of listening to the reassuring sounds of her grandmother methodically going through the motions of putting dishes away, getting ready for bed then turning lights off. Finally overcome by exhaustion, Quinn fell sound asleep.

The hours led into days and the days led into later the following week. Quinn hadn't showered, had barely eaten anything and rarely got out of bed for more than an hour at a time. Occasionally she heard her mobile ring but ignored it. She wasn't in the mood to speak to anyone.

"Go the fuck away!" she screamed out as it rang, yet again. "I don't want to talk to any of you!" She grabbed the phone, unplugging it from its charger as she did. Looking at it she saw that it was her mother calling this time. She saw that François and Darcy had also called multiple times each.

"Go the hell away." Slamming the phone back down on the night table it slipped off and fell under the bed. Reaching for it without success, Quinn gave up trying. Pulling the quilt over her head, she just wanted to sleep and shut the world out. It was dusk so she decided to just stay in bed and go to sleep.

● ● ●

Startled awake by the sound of banging at the front door, Quinn awoke to darkness. Still half asleep she darted out of bed.

Who could that be?

Not thinking to turn a light on, she headed for the front door but had forgotten about her suitcases still sitting out in the middle of the hallway where she had dropped them almost a week and a half ago with the intention of putting them into the closet. Proceeding to trip over them, she landed hard onto the floor, yelling out in pain as she hit her head on the hall table on her way down.

"Owww! Dammit!"

Again, banging on the door, this time louder and with more intensity.

"Yes, I'm coming, I'm coming!"

Slowly standing back up, she quickly headed to the front hall, turned on the light and opened the door.

"Yes?!" she was out of breath and annoyed.

TWENTY

L ooking up, Quinn was less than pleased by the sight of Darcy standing in front of her.

."Oh. It's you. Feel free to turn around and leave because I want nothing to do with you." Turning to walk away, she heard him follow her in and shut the door. Stopping, she turned and glared at him. "What the hell are you doing here anyway and why aren't you leaving?" She was in no mood to make nice and quite frankly was angry that the cheating bastard had the nerve to show up on her doorstep at all let alone when all she wanted was to be left alone.

Hesitating he had a look of concern on his face and asked, "Um…are you okay?"

"What?! Why wouldn't I be?" Quinn sounded as irritated as she actually was.

."Are you sure you're okay?"

"Yes, I'm okay! Why do you even care, anyway?"

."Really? Well, besides the fact that you look a complete wreck, you have a cut on your head and you're bleeding." He said matter-of-factly making no attempt to help her.

"I'm what?!" Quickly turning to look in the mirror in the front hall, Quinn was shocked to see blood dripping down her face and now onto the sweater she was wearing over her pajamas.

"Oh, shit!" Running down the hall to the washroom, Quinn searched for band-aids but could not immediately find any so she grabbed the hand towel off the rack and pressed it to her head. Turning to return to the front door, Quinn was annoyed to see Darcy standing in the doorway of the washroom.

"Why are you here? I want you to leave right now." *François is going to get a piece of my mind when I see him. Why would he give Darcy directions here when he knows very well I want nothing to do with him.*

"I'm glad to see you, too!" He replied sarcastically. "Now, can I help you with that cut?"

"No! I don't need any fucking help! Least of all from you!" Quinn replied defensively, angrier than ever.

"Okay." Stopping to think for a moment, Darcy continued, "Well then, I must tell you that you've got everything all wrong, you know."

"I don't know what the hell you're talking about." Quinn refused to make eye contact. She was completely disoriented, unsure of the time, let alone what day it was.

"Don't play games with me, Quinn. You know exactly what I'm talking about and you've got it all wrong."

"Fine then, but I know what I heard and she very clearly said that you have a wife!"

"I don't have a wife."

"Oh sure! That's what *you* say, but that...what's her name, whoever answered your phone, said that you do."

"Well, you heard wrong. I was on stage giving a speech with the *owner* and *his* wife for a charity event. The owner of a building my sister's company built and the person who answered the phone was my sister. Now, will you please let me help you with that cut?"

Quinn tried to absorb what Darcy had just said.

"I don't believe you." Her anger softened slightly as she spoke.

"What's not to believe? I have the newspaper article I can show you if you need proof but believe me when I say, I am not married."

Quinn was trying to get her mind thinking clearly but was finding it difficult. She felt tired but shouldn't have been given the amount of sleep she'd had since she arrived at the cabin. She just couldn't shake the lightheadedness she felt. Still holding the towel to her head, she looked up at Darcy.

"So, no wife?" she asked sheepishly.

"No wife," he reassured her. "Now, please let me look at that cut."

Pulling the towel away from her head, she cringed at the sight of the blood. Looking in the mirror, she was shocked by what she saw, although she wouldn't have admitted it. Not only was her forehead still bleeding profusely, she couldn't overlook the pathetic sight of herself. *Darcy was right, she looked a complete wreck.* Her hair was greasy looking, matted with the bedhead look to an extreme. She had smudges of mascara under her eyes, her clothes were actually quite revolting looking with food stains on the sweater that she wore. It was then she realized that she was still wearing the same pajamas she had worn since arriving. *Oh well, I don't even care*, she thought as she applied more pressure in the hopes her forehead would stop bleeding.

Sitting on the side of the tub, she asked, "So why are you here, anyway?"

"First of all, let me fix up your head. Do you have any band-aids and rubbing alcohol?"

Giving him an impatient look, Quinn turned her attention to finding band-aids.

"I have no idea. They are usually kept in the cabinet here, but I don't see them and I'm perfectly capable of doing it myself, thank you very much."

"Here, let me look for them. Keep the pressure on it. Even minor cuts on the head tend to bleed like a son of a bitch."

Quinn waited patiently while Darcy searched through the cupboards until he found both band-aids and rubbing alcohol.

"Here we go. Now, let me take a look at that." Pulling the towel away from her forehead, he turned the tap on and wet a corner of the towel then began to carefully wipe the blood off Quinn's forehead. "How did this happen?" he asked.

She felt a little uncomfortable but was admittedly enjoying being taken care of. Closing her eyes, she felt him wipe her forehead clean. Opening them again, she watched as he poured rubbing alcohol onto a cotton ball and cringed when he dabbed it on her cut. She was beginning to feel a bit self-conscious about her appearance the more she woke up.

"I tripped over my suitcases in the hallway as I was running to answer the door." She almost felt like a little kid sitting there being tended to.

Grabbing a band-aid, Darcy pulled it open and carefully placed it over the cut, then inspected his work.

"And you didn't think to turn on the light?" Darcy pushed.

"No, I didn't think to turn on the light! I was half asleep. What do you expect?"

Disregarding the question, Darcy said, "There. Luckily you don't need stitches. That should take care of it. Do you have a headache? Feel dizzy at all?"

"No…well I did, but I don't now." she responded self-consciously.

"Okay then." Staring at Quinn, Darcy seemed to linger just a little longer than necessary and then cleared his throat. "You'll be fine. I've used a waterproof band-aid so you can shower now."

"But I'm not showering."

"Yes, you are." Darcy firmly responded.

Glaring at him she repeated again, "I said, I'm not showering."

"Oh, but you are," he said unwaveringly. He knew Quinn wasn't going to win this battle but was clearly getting the impression that *she* didn't understand that she wasn't going to win on this and that she would require a little help seeing things his way.

"I said, I'm not!" she was getting angrier by the minute. "There is nothing wrong with the way I look." She knew that was a blatant lie but crossed her arms in defiance.

"Really? Well you look like hell and you smell no better, now get in that shower." Darcy was calm but adamant. He knew he was being hurtful but also knew Quinn clearly wasn't herself.

Reaching behind her, he turned the shower on and let it warm up. "Get in."

"No! I won't!" Quinn stood her ground. "Who said you have the right to come into my grandmoth...*my* cabin and tell me what I should and shouldn't be doing? I am not taking a shower! I don't feel like it. I'm tired. I need to go back to bed."

Darcy stood his ground.

"Let me be perfectly clear. You *are* having a shower and you're having a shower on your own or I'm putting you in there and showering you myself but I can assure you that you are having a shower." Darcy wasn't angry. He knew in the end he would get his way.

"Good luck getting me in there because I have no intention of showering!" Quinn stood up, arms still crossed in front of her. "And you can't make me!" She screamed like an insolent child. Turning around to turn the shower off, Quinn suddenly felt Darcy grab her around the waist with both his arms, then lift her into the shower, clothes and all. He too was fully dressed and getting wet but he didn't care and held her under the water stream.

"Get the fuck off of me you...you...bully! How dare you! What gives you the right..." she angrily shouted as she spit water out of her mouth.

"The fact that you stink and look like hell," he cruelly offered.

Taking a shocked breath in and coughing on the cascading water, Quinn couldn't believe what she was hearing.

"How dare you!" Still struggling, she could feel him pour something on her head and start roughly scrubbing her hair. She presumed shampoo by the smell of it.

"Ow! Be careful! You're hurting me!"

"Well, are you going to do this on your own or do I need to carry on?"

Angry beyond belief, Quinn relented to the fact that she wasn't going to win this argument.

"Okay, okay, I'll shower myself now get the hell out of here!"

Stepping out of the shower, Darcy chuckled as he saw Quinn give him a dirty look and angrily close the shower curtain in his face.

"You're an asshole, you know that?!" she shouted out unable to resist getting the last word in but grew even angrier when she heard Darcy laughing.

In a few moments her wet clothes were being flung out onto the washroom floor, piece by piece. Satisfied that she was going to stay put and get cleaned up, Darcy dried himself off as best he could and left the room, shutting the door quietly behind him.

TWENTY ONE

*H*aving changed into dry clothes, Darcy sat in the living room enjoying a glass of wine, appreciating the warm fire he had started as he waited for Quinn to emerge from the washroom.

"You didn't have to do that you know."

Looking up, he saw Quinn standing glaring at him, dressed in clean pajamas and wearing a cardigan sweater. Her hair was wet but brushed, dangling down around her shoulders and her eyes were void of any mascara smudges. He was pleased to see that she looked much better than when he first saw her but she still looked fatigued.

"Oh, yeah, I did." he assured her with a grin and took another sip of wine. "You want some?"

Frowning she mumbled, "Yes," then added, "...but I'm still mad at you."

"I can live with that. Okay, sit down here by the fire I took the liberty of starting. I'll get you a glass." He felt sorry for her but wasn't about to coddle her. "When did you eat last?"

"This morning...I think...I don't know." She was having trouble thinking clearly. Timelines were all melded together. She really wasn't sure if she last ate that day or the day before.

"Ok, I'll be back. Sit down."

Quinn could hear Darcy working about in the kitchen but she was too tired to wonder what he was doing. She had to admit that she felt much better after taking a shower.

Sitting staring into the fire, she didn't think of anything in particular except that she was, in fact, appreciating the warmth and comfort emanating from it. Closing her eyes, she rested her head back onto the chair, enjoying listening to the crackling sounds and the smell of the wood burning. A smell that took her back over the years to when she was a little girl and her grandfather would build fires at night, with her snuggling on his lap, wrapped in a blanket, feeling the love and safety nestled in his arms.

She must have dosed off because, in what seemed like just a few moments, Darcy had returned and was standing there with a tray of food and a glass of wine for her.

"What's this?" she asked. The food not only looked good but it smelled just as divine.

"It's chili with some sour cream and grated cheddar cheese on it. I actually found the chili in the freezer."

"Oh, well, I'm not really that hungry, thanks. You can have it." She grabbed the wine and turned away looking back into the fire.

"I don't care if you're hungry or not, you're eating it." Darcy was firm.

"I said I'm not hungry," she insisted.

"You're eating. Now here." Darcy forced the tray in her direction and stood there waiting for her to take it.

Sighing heavily, Quinn was too tired to argue. "Okay, fine. I'll eat." She felt defeated. There was no reason for her to feel this way but everything seemed so overwhelming these days.

Sitting back down in the other easy chair, Darcy stared into the fire, sipped on his wine and said nothing but was pleased when he finally saw Quinn eating.

As much as she hated to admit it, Quinn felt ravished and couldn't eat fast enough. She always did love her grandmother's chili and this was exactly what she needed right now, although she didn't really want to admit that to Darcy.

Chapter TWENTY ONE

After finishing her food, Quinn set the tray on the floor beside her chair and sipped on the wine. She couldn't bring herself to say anything. She didn't want to talk and was grateful that Darcy didn't speak to her.

Finishing her wine, Quinn could feel herself relax and the stress on her body seemed to diminish. Closing her eyes once again, she found herself drifting off and before she knew it, she felt herself being picked up by Darcy, carried into the bedroom and placed into bed. The sheets smelled fresh and she smiled as she felt him cover her up and kiss her on the cheek as he quietly whispered, "Good night, Quinn. Sleep well," before she drifted off to sleep.

TWENTY TWO

*T*he next morning, Quinn awoke to the sun shining on her face and taking a few moments to wake up, she tried to get her bearings. Lying there she felt content…happy, although she couldn't explain why. Hearing noises in the kitchen, she knew it would be Darcy but for a few brief moments she wanted to pretend that it was her grandmother. The sadness washed over her once again but this time it didn't stay. This time she felt compelled to get out of bed and greet the day.

Having gone to the washroom, Quinn brushed her teeth and her hair, then wandered down to the kitchen, stopping in the doorway she shook her head and smiled as she watched the scene that was unfolding before her.

Darcy had her grandmother's apron on and was busy cooking bacon and making coffee. In moments, the toast popped up out of the toaster and he methodically brushed it with butter and placed it on a plate in the oven to stay warm. When he opened the oven door, Quinn noticed he had made pancakes and her heart skipped a beat. He could have been her grandmother in disguise. Quinn was grateful for this moment and didn't want to disturb it but, unfortunately, Darcy saw her, looked up and smiled.

"Good morning, Sunshine! How did you sleep?" He stood, frying pan in one hand and a butter knife in the other.

"Good thanks."

"Glad to hear it." And with that, he proceeded to place the pan on the stove and cracked some eggs into it. "Have a seat at the table. The breakfast of your life is about to be served."

Sitting down, Quinn was thankful to have a coffee placed in front of her. Sipping it, she closed her eyes and took in the aroma. Next thing she knew there was a plate with two eggs in front of her and Darcy was setting out plates of bacon, pancakes and toast onto the table. Watching him pour them each a glass of juice, Quinn smiled to see that the pancakes were blueberry.

She hadn't felt this cared for in a very long time and she was feeling a bit emotional.

Sitting down, Darcy looked up at her and seeing tears in her eyes, asked, "What? Did I forget something?"

Quinn was too choked up to answer and quietly shook her head.

Darcy said nothing at first, then offered, "Eat up! Don't let it get cold."

Nodding, Quinn helped herself to pancakes and bacon. Eating everything up quickly she added more food to her plate. It was all so delicious and the pancakes tasted exactly like her grandmother's.

"Everything is delicious, Darcy, thank you." Quinn was beginning to feel more human than she had in a couple of weeks.

"My pleasure and I hope you don't mind but I found your grandmother's cookbook and used her recipe for the pancakes. I would never have added vanilla but I must admit it adds a nice touch to them and there were berries in the freezer." Darcy said as he ate his breakfast.

Quinn smiled thinking about how impressed her grandmother would have been to meet Darcy and see how handy he was in the kitchen.

"I thought they tasted like hers." Quinn looked up and said, "Darcy…"

Looking at Quinn, he waited for her to continue.

"Thank you."

Shrugging, Darcy said, "No problem," then continued eating.

"And, I'm sorry...I shouldn't have made an assumption..." Quinn felt ashamed as she spoke. "I should have given you the benefit of the doubt."

"Yes, you should have." Darcy responded matter-of-factly as he took another bite of his pancakes.

"I wasn't thinking clearly. I was a mess about my grandmother... anyway, there's no excuse..." Her voice drifted off.

"That's true, you weren't thinking." He was teasing her to lighten the mood but added, "Forget about it. Next time, give me a chance to defend myself. I deserve that at least."

"You do, and fair enough." She felt embarrassed but was too worn out to dwell on it.

Darcy stopped eating and affectionately looked at Quinn. He sat quietly for a moment as he saw tears come to her eyes.

"François told me about your grandmother."

Nodding, Quinn realized that she hadn't mentioned anything about her grandmother to Darcy.

"I'm devastated, Darcy. She was my biggest champion in this world and I don't know what I'm ever going to do without her." Quinn's voice was emotional and drifted off as she spoke.

"No one loved me like she did." Looking out the window Quinn sat quietly, deep in thought.

"Quinn, the only person who really needs to love you, is you." Darcy spoke quietly.

Looking back at him through tear-filled eyes, Quinn couldn't speak.

"It doesn't matter what your parents, sister, this Spencer guy, thought or thinks..."

"How do you know about Spencer or my family?" Then she realized. "Of course...François."

"It doesn't matter about any of them. You lost your grandmother but you still have François, who, by the way, is a pretentious snob but a damned good friend,' he laughed and was pleased when he saw her smile.

"And you have..." hesitating, he added, "...me. You have me too, Quinn."

She sat quietly, tears streaming down her face as she looked around the familiar kitchen.

"So, why are you crying? Is my cooking that bad?" he joked.

Laughing through her tears, she responded, "No, no, this is the best breakfast I've had in a very long time and especially since I've been here." Wiping away her tears, Quinn was a little uncomfortable revealing her vulnerability to Darcy but strangely, felt relieved. She hadn't known him long but she felt...safe...and dare she think, loved.

Taking a sip of his coffee, Darcy watched her carefully.

"Thank you for what you've done for me."

"Quinn, you don't need to thank me for anything."

"Yes. Yes, I do. I clearly wasn't doing well. Thank you. I'm feeling better today."

Smiling slightly, he said, "You're welcome but you can thank François because he's the one who called me. He phoned yesterday morning, explained what was going on. He wanted to give you space to deal with things here but then became worried when he couldn't get a hold of you...we both were. He was going to come but I told him I would and I was happy to." Thinking for a moment, he continued, "It's been a couple of weeks, Quinn."

"I dunno...I was so upset and my parents didn't help matters. Then everything with you...I was just overwhelmed, I guess..."

"Understandable." Sitting in silence for a few moments, Darcy said, "Well, you'll feel even better after we go for a walk today." Knowing he could get some resistance, he was preparing his response.

Chapter TWENTY TWO

"Walk?" Quinn looked up at him.

"Yup! Now that you've had a shower you won't attract any animals…" he teased. "You were pretty rough looking…and smelling," he chuckled at her expense.

"Yeah." Embarrassed, she sat quietly for a moment, then added, "I don't really feel up to going for a walk today, though. Maybe tomorrow." She still felt tired and just wanted to stay put. "I think I'll take a nap this afternoon instead."

"Ah, but, no you won't. You're coming for a walk with me and I won't take no for an answer." Darcy insisted. "The fresh air will do you some good."

"But…"

"No buts, Quinn. You're getting out and getting some fresh air and exercise. I'm sure you've slept enough to last a lifetime. You can show me around this beautiful property of yours."

Sighing, Quinn reluctantly agreed to go. "Alright! But I'm having a nap when I get back."

"Deal." Darcy grinned. "Now go get dressed."

She was annoyed but got up and headed to the bedroom to change.

TWENTY THREE

Stepping outside was like a shock to the system for Quinn. She hadn't been out since she arrived almost two weeks prior and didn't realize how cold it had gotten. There was more snow on the ground than she realized. The sun was shining brightly causing the fresh snow to glisten. Putting her sunglasses on, she took in a deep breath of fresh air and started walking, hearing the snow crunching beneath her boots with every step she took.

The time went quickly. She took Darcy down to the lake to where they used to jump into the water by a rope swing, then to her grandfather's large workshop at the bottom of the hill and finally back up to the cabin. In total they walked for a couple of hours and she had to admit she felt invigorated. She and Darcy talked the entire way about nothing of importance. He made her laugh and that's exactly what she needed.

Walking along the path to the front of the cabin, Quinn realized Darcy had become very quiet. Turning to see where he was she was taken aback by the shock of a snowball hitting her in the face.

"Ahhh! Oh my God, you did not just do that!" she shouted as she wiped the snow from her face.

"Oh, but I did!" Darcy laughed as he bent over to make another snowball.

"Game on, Mr. Monaghan!" But before she could make a snowball herself, she was pelted with another one.

Grabbing some snow in her hands, she ducked to miss a third and threw one at Darcy, hitting him smack in the middle of the chest.

Quickly hiding behind a bush beside the path, Quinn made another snowball and peeked over the bush to see where he was and was hit again with cold snow.

"Oh, you're going down!" she hollered out and threw another snowball in his direction, this time hitting him on the forehead. "Gotcha!" she yelled, pleased with her aim disregarding the fact that she really hadn't aimed at all.

Seeing Darcy run towards her, Quinn squealed and started running across the yard as fast as she could through the snow and away from him but he caught up to her quickly, tackling her face down into the freshly fallen snow.

Trying to escape, she wiggled free and crawled her way along the ground without much success. Darcy grabbed her legs and flipped her over onto her back. Quickly grabbing a handful of snow, he gently smeared it all over her face. Quinn spit the snow out of her mouth, wiping her face. Laughing, they both stopped to look at each other and said nothing. Slowly leaning down, Darcy kissed Quinn gently on the lips. Quinn reciprocated much more passionately, releasing all the emotion of the last few weeks. Feeling more loved in that solitary kiss than she had her entire lifetime, she decided that she wasn't going to hold back any longer. It was time she started to live again.

Heading back into the cabin, they took their coats and boots off and overcome with emotion Quinn kissed Darcy. She wanted to cry and yet was exhilarated and allowed every passionate emotion to flow. It was like the floodgates opened up and she lost complete control.

In moments she felt him pick her up and carry her to the bedroom, gently placing her on the bed. Quinn couldn't say a word and closed her eyes as she felt him gently reach for the waistband of her track pants and ever so slowly pull them down while simultaneously kissing different parts of her body, softly, every inch of the way…her tummy, her hips, her legs, her toes. Pulling them off, Darcy tossed them to the floor then reached for her panties, slowly pulling them down and as he kissed her just below the waist she quietly moaned aloud. Gently spreading her legs apart with his hands, Darcy reached down with his fingers and slowly began caressing her. She was utterly breathless. Momentarily stopping, he undressed quickly then kneeling down slid his hands under her bottom elevating her just enough to better reach the front of her with his warm, exploring tongue. Feeling the warmth and slow massaging motion between her legs Quinn caught her breath. Keeping her eyes closed she couldn't think of anything else but the tingling sensation she felt over her entire body. Within moments her body shuddered in gratitude and arrived at a place she hadn't been in a very long time and just as she thought she couldn't have felt any better, Quinn felt Darcy slowly pull her sweatshirt up revealing her naked breasts then felt his tongue methodically work it's way over and around, exploring every part of her nipples creating an overwhelming sensation of ecstasy. Quinn just laid there with her arms above her head falling victim to his tenderness, feeling herself reaching a point of no return once again. Slowly breathing in and then out Quinn found it hard to remain silent. She was almost in a trance as she focused on Darcy suckling on her nipples while moving his tongue over each one, slowly, tenderly. Feeling him slide gently into her she took in a deep breath as she enjoyed his long, slow, firm movements in and then out. Quinn felt uninhibited passion as they shuddered together in blissful ecstasy. Feeling Darcy pull away then lay down beside her, Quinn was enjoying every second of this physical, passionate relationship. Beads of sweat rolling down her face, her body felt drained yet her senses were heightened. She was in a blissful stupor.

Thank you, God! Quinn couldn't think straight, couldn't speak.

"Quinn?" she heard Darcy whisper several moments later.

Finally able to catch her breath, Quinn said, "Yeah?"

"You okay?"

"Oh, yeah." *That's an understatement.*

Lying in Darcy's arms, Quinn looked out the bedroom window, admiring the blue sky and snow resting gently on the trees. Sighing contentedly, she slid her hand gently across Darcy's chest, feeling his smooth skin and the rhythmic movement of his chest with every breath he took. She couldn't believe how, in just a day, her feelings could be transformed from all-consuming anger, grief and sadness to happiness and contentment. *How could Darcy have known exactly what I needed at the most depressed time of my life?*

Looking up she thought, *Grandma, I'm not sure how you knew to send him when you did, but thank you. You always did know how to make me feel better.* Quinn smiled at the thought of her grandmother. Such a nice change from the tears she had almost incessantly shed since her death.

Wrapping his arms tightly around Quinn, Darcy leaned in and kissed her.

"Well? We've managed to spend the afternoon here in this bedroom and as much as I would love to stay here, I think we should be getting up before our company arrives."

Quinn looked at Darcy in surprise. "What company?"

"François. I called and asked him to come up overnight."

Smiling, Quinn couldn't have thought of a more perfect way to spend the weekend and grew excited at the thought of seeing her friend.

"How did you manage to convince him to come here? He hates anywhere but the city."

"It wasn't easy but it was all in the name of you needing your best friend to support you and although he was reluctant, I managed to show him how important it was that he come."

Laughing, Quinn was impressed with Darcy's convincing ways.

"When will he be here?" she asked as she crawled out of bed and put on some clothes.

"He was going to leave work early to get here by roughly six o'clock. He said he wanted a spaghetti dinner."

Quinn had to admit she was looking forward to preparing dinner but stopped, "But I don't have the ingredients I need."

"François is bringing them. He said he knew what you needed." Darcy assured her.

• ● •

The time surprisingly went by quickly and it wasn't long before they heard a car pull up. Peeking out the front window Quinn saw François and instantly became excited. Running to the front door to greet her friend, Quinn opened it.

"Oh my God, François, I'm so glad you came!"

Dropping his overnight bag onto the floor, François gave Quinn a big hug with a wave to Darcy standing behind her.

"Oh my God, Q! Do you realize how worried I was about you? I couldn't get a hold of you! You didn't call! What the fuck was I to think? I mean, you could have been dead out here for all I knew. I was relieved to hear from Darcy that you were fine. What the hell were you thinking not staying in touch when you are all by yourself out in fucking no-man's land?"

"François! You knew why I was coming here and that I needed a break. Why would you worry?"

"Well, I expected you to at least call to say when you were coming home and when you wouldn't return any of my calls, which isn't like you, I called Darcy. What's a person to think?" François reasoned. "I almost called in the RCMP."

"Well, I'm fine. Okay, well, it's true, I wasn't fine but I am now thanks to Darcy and really, thanks to you, too."

"Well, don't ever do that again. You have no idea how close I was to calling in the Mounties to look for you. You wouldn't believe the lies I had to tell your mother…every…fucking…time she called me. Remind me to change my mobile number. I can't take it anymore! I've told you before that she's like a fucking bloodhound on a scent asking all those questions she asks! I honestly don't think she believed me, anyway."

Quinn and Darcy laughed as they listened to François rant.

"Good God, I didn't realize how fucking remote this place is! Are you absolutely sure you want to keep it?"

"Yes, I do. You know that I love it here! I won't be living here full time anyway and besides you will grow to love it here, too!"

"The hell I will! You will never see me up here again. It's so fucking cold out and there's even that horrible white stuff on the ground," he exaggerated. "My God! It's barely November!" François took off his cashmere overcoat along with his hat and leather gloves.

"Jesus! These are fine Italian leather shoes and they have snow all over them! How was I supposed to know there would be snow on the ground? I mean, honestly, how could I have known to bring boots with me? My God! Do you have a soft cloth I can use to dry them off before they are ruined? Unfucking believable!" Removing his shoes, he waited for Darcy to leave and return with something to dry them off. "We have no snow at all back home!" he muttered.

Chuckling, Quinn and Darcy watched as he carefully wiped his shoes down, ensuring every last drop of snow was removed. It seemed to take forever.

"Are you done yet?" Quinn laughed.

"Listen, Q, I will support you through all of this country living shit but by God I won't ruin imported Italian leather shoes for anyone." Pointing towards a brown paper bag, Quinn looked inside and smiled when she saw two bottles of red wine.

"You sure know the way to a girl's heart, François!"

"And there's food in those bags." He pointed to two other bags sitting on the floor.

Quinn knew he hated any accommodations less than five star but she also knew that he would do just about anything for her because as tough as he talked, he was a big 'ole softie inside and she loved him for that.

"Come into the kitchen. I'll crack one of these bottles open and start making spaghetti."

Quinn could hear Darcy and François speaking in the hall before they headed down to the kitchen. Pouring them each some wine, she handed a glass to both men as they entered the kitchen then watched as they sat down and began to talk. *My two favourite men. How lucky am I?*

Quinn loved listening to the warm conversation and the life it brought to the cabin. It felt like a different place than it had two weeks ago, even a few days ago. Her grandmother would have loved that. It made Quinn happy.

TWENTY FOUR

"**O**h my God, Q, I love your spaghetti. I really should have been born Italian." François pushed his plate away after he finished the last of his meal.

"I have to agree with François. You really do make the best spaghetti. Even I couldn't do any better." Darcy teased as he winked at Quinn, who playfully stuck her tongue out at him.

"Well, thank you gentleman. I appreciate the compliments." Quinn cleared the table and then checked to see if her grandmother had any cookies in the freezer. Her specialties were chocolate chip and oatmeal raisin and she had often kept tins of cookies in the freezer for when company came to visit. Digging deep down, she found the tin she was looking for.

"Okay boys we have dessert, compliments of Esther." Placing the tin in the middle of the kitchen table, Quinn quickly pulled the lid off and was happy to see it was filled with chocolate chip cookies. *Thank you, Grandma.*

"Let's go into the living room and enjoy the fire, then maybe you guys would like to play a board game. There aren't many here but there are a few. There is definitely Monopoly"

"No! No! No! I am absolutely not playing Monopoly with you, Q!" François was firm.

"Why? What's wrong with Monopoly?" Darcy was curious to know.

Quinn laughed out loud. "Oh, François! Don't be such a poor sport. You see, Darcy, nothing is wrong with Monopoly, I love the game, but the last time we played I managed to bankrupt him...well actually... every time we play I beat him and what you don't know about François is that he hates to lose."

Darcy nodded his head with understanding. "I could see that," he laughed.

"Boasting doesn't become you, Q." François pouted.

"And pouting doesn't become you." she laughed.

"Okay you two, we can play another game, stop fighting." Darcy teased.

"I still don't understand your obsession with bloody board games, Q, but fine I'll play anything but Monopoly. God knows I could think of a thousand other things I would rather do but all of those involve being in the city with a cute guy, a nightclub and expensive wine and clearly there is none of that to be found in this God-forsaken countryside," he muttered feigning feeling sorry for himself, "...except of course, the expensive wine that I thankfully brought. You're welcome." Taking a sip of wine, François ignored Quinn and Darcy as they laughed.

As the evening progressed, Quinn could feel herself relaxing more and more and realized that keeping the cabin was a good idea. She wasn't sure how she was going to do it but she would worry about that later. First she needed to get a job. *Or win the lottery,* she thought with a chuckle.

Playing a different board game proved to be just as frustrating for François so when he finally lost he sat back in the kitchen chair brooding.

"Anyway, I'm glad I lost the damn game because now I can just sit and drink."

"Don't worry, François. She's kicking my ass too." Darcy tried to sooth François' bruised ego.

"So, Quinn. What have you decided about keeping this place?" François asked.

"I'm going to keep it. All I need is to get a job and start bringing in some money and I'm sure I will manage." Quinn felt more positive than ever before.

"Why do you need money?" Darcy instantly became concerned. "Maybe I can help."

Seeing the look on his face, Quinn wanted to be perfectly clear, "Listen, Darcy. It's nothing I can't handle and I don't want you thinking I'm looking for any financial assistance. This place needs some small repairs, that's all."

"Some! That's an understatement!" François interrupted, shocked at how his friend was trying to downplay the repairs needed.

Darcy looked from François back to Quinn. "Why? Is there a lot of work needed here because I know someone in the business."

"No, no. It's all good. I don't need help." Quinn contended.

"But I know someone in the business who might be able to help." Darcy once again offered.

"No. It will be fine. Really." Quinn wasn't completely convinced herself but she certainly didn't want to involve Darcy in her problems with the cabin.

"Give up, Darcy. She's stubborn." François muttered as he put his feet up on the ottoman in front of him.

Wrapping up the game, Quinn told the guys she was heading to bed and said goodnight. Lying in bed, the smell of the fire was relaxing. Smiling, she listened to the men talking and laughing. It was a sound she found comforting. She couldn't hear what they were talking about, just that there were a few minutes of conversation followed by laughter. One of them went to the kitchen, opened the fridge and by the sound of things, poured more wine into a glass before walking back to the living room. She could hear logs being thrown onto the fire, then more conversation. It did her heart good knowing that her boyfriend and her best friend got along so well. Quinn wasn't exactly sure when she fell asleep, she just knew that she felt at peace and happy when she did.

TWENTY FIVE

The next morning she awoke to Darcy asleep beside her and snoring. She was surprised that she hadn't heard him come to bed but acknowledged that she had, in fact, slept very well. Lying there, deep in thought, Quinn acknowledged that it was time to go back home. She was still heartbroken at the loss of her grandmother but she no longer felt emotionally paralyzed with grief. She felt better prepared to face her loss and was grateful to Darcy and François for helping her get there.

Quietly crawling out of bed, she threw on her housecoat and slippers then headed down to the kitchen where she turned the kettle on. Seeing the array of wine bottles, she laughed. *Clearly those boys were up late last night.* They had not only finished the two bottles of wine François brought with him but two others as well and some beer, judging by the empty beer bottles lingering about. *Well, I suspect they won't be in the mood for much food this morning,* she smiled as she started gathering empties.

"Well Grandma, you would be so happy right now. You always did enjoy having young people around, as you would put it. What would you say? 'Keeps me young at heart, Quinn, and I would much rather be around you and your friends than those ole stick-in-the-mud parents of yours.'"

Wiping the counters down, Quinn washed dishes, then made herself some coffee and headed into the living room. Making a fire with some of the wood Darcy had brought in, Quinn sat down in her grandmother's chair and enjoyed the peace and quiet. She had been so sad to come here and now she was reluctant to leave.

"Well, I see you are quite adept at making fires."

Looking up, Quinn smiled as Darcy trudged into the room, shirtless. *François would go crazy if he was seeing this.* She watched as he sat down in her grandfather's chair in front of the fire.

"Want a coffee?" she asked, knowing full well he would need one after the amount of drinking that seemingly took place the night before.

"Ah, yeah, that would be good. Thanks." Darcy had a t-shirt in hand and put it on as he sat there.

Quinn smirked as she saw that he had, in fact, put the shirt on inside out.

"Rough morning, Darcy?" she teased.

"Yeah, I'd say so." then added, "That François can sure handle his own when drinking. My God, I had a hard time keeping up with him."

"I think it's the French blood in him. He seems to be able to hold his own quite well when it comes to drinking wine, not so much anything else though. Be right back, I'll grab your coffee."

Returning a few minutes later, Quinn handed Darcy the coffee which he gratefully accepted. Leaning back in the chair, he quietly sipped on it, then placed his head back on the chair, eyes closed.

"Want some breakfast?" Quinn was pretty sure she knew the answer.

"I think I should stay away from food for a while."

"Perhaps you need a walk to clear your head?" She was poking fun at him but couldn't resist.

'I think I'll pass on that right now as well."

"Okay." Looking up, she smirked at the sight of François walking into the living room looking as hung over as one could look.

In the perkiest voice she could possibly muster, she said, "Good morning, François! How are you this fine morning? Would you like some breakfast?"

"Fuck off, Q," was all he could muster before sitting down.

Chapter TWENTY FIVE

"Aw, did you boys have a bit too much to drink last night?"

Saying nothing, François and Darcy just sat with their eyes closed.

"Well, I'm going back to bed." Darcy said.

"Me too." François seconded.

Quinn could only laugh as she watched them both disappear from the living room. *Well, I guess I'll start packing up to go home and with any luck we will be able to get out of here before dark but God knows with the shape those two are in.*

TWENTY SIX

*B*y three o'clock Quinn was happy to see Darcy reappear from the bedroom looking much better than he had earlier.

Walking into the kitchen, he noticed she was sitting having a cup of herbal tea and some food.

"What's that you're eating?"

"Just some cheese, crackers, fruit and veggies. Do you want some?"

"Is there any spaghetti left over?" Darcy craved something a little more fulfilling after not having any food since the night before.

"Sure! I'll warm some up for you."

Placing some spaghetti on a plate and putting it into the microwave to warm up, she turned to see Darcy pouring himself a cup of tea.

"Feeling a bit better than you were this morning? That was some night the two of you had."

"Yeah, to say the least. That François drank me under the table." Darcy smiled at the thought.

"Yes, I should have forewarned you."

"Well, I finally gave up on wine and started drinking beer. I suppose that was my downfall really. Shouldn't have mixed drinks like that. I know better."

"Or perhaps it was the *amount* you drank?" Quinn teased.

Hearing the beeps of the microwave, Quinn pulled the plate of spaghetti out and placed it and a fork in front of Darcy.

"Is he up yet?" Darcy asked as he dug into the hot meal.

"Not yet but I'll be getting him up soon. I'm sure he'll want to get on the road especially since it's snowing again today."

"Yes, because his sports car will get all wet and dirty with this weather." Darcy joked between bites.

"It's too bad we are all driving separate vehicles." Quinn didn't look forward to the long drive home alone but she was used to it after all the years of coming to the cabin.

"Oh my God, I can't believe you're eating that." François stood in the kitchen doorway staring at the two sitting eating at the kitchen table. "I don't think I could eat a thing right now."

"That's what you get when you drink too much." Quinn lovingly scolded. "I can't remember the last time you had that much to drink, François."

"It's all Darcy's fault. He just kept pouring those fucking drinks."

Laughing Darcy reminded, "Aw c'mon now, François. It wasn't like I was pouring them down your throat, now."

"Yeah, whatever. Oh my God, I've got a vicious headache." Sitting down at the table, François picked up a piece of cheese from Quinn's plate and ate it.

"Perhaps if you drink water or something and have some food you will feel better. It's a long drive home when you're hung over." Quinn offered.

"I suppose. Maybe just some of what you have, Q. That's enough."

"Sure." Sliding her plate in François' direction, she smiled as she watched him painstakingly eat.

"I've packed everything up except food from the fridge. Is there anything else either of you want?"

Both men shook their heads no.

Chapter TWENTY SIX

"I'll likely be back here soon anyway because I will need to go through my grandmother's things and decide what to do with them, not to mention, set aside everything my grandmother willed to the rest of my family so I can take it home with me." Standing up, Quinn stopped for a moment.

"Listen…" She hesitated before continuing. "I just want to say thank you for caring about me as much as you do. If it wasn't for you both I would have likely still been here drowning in my sorrows." She was uncomfortable expressing how she felt but knew she had to say what was on her mind. "It's just…"

"For God's sake, woman, I've got a fucking headache. I can't take this right now." François moaned.

"Geez François, I'm about to pour my heart out here." Quinn pleaded.

"Christ, Q, it was no big deal. You would have done the same for us. What the hell are friends for if not to drag each other's sorry asses out of the gutter and back onto their feet from time to time." François was impatient. He really didn't want this conversation right now.

"François!" Quinn frowned at her friend.

"Oh my God, fine! Don't you remember last year when I broke up with…what the hell was his name?" Shaking his head, François continued, "Anyway, it doesn't matter. You were the one who found me at work at something like midnight, pissed drunk and crying on the floor in the washroom. What did you do then? You took me home, put me to bed and stayed with me all night long…"

"And then gave you proper shit the next day for going out with such a daft idiot to begin with. You knew he was married and yet you still put yourself in the way of heartbreak. I wasn't exactly patient with you about it." Quinn remembered how hurt her friend had been and although she had scolded him at the time, her heart had broken for him.

"Regardless, you kicked my ass and got me back on track again. You were the only one who could." François continued to pick at the food.

Darcy was sympathetic. "Quinn, it was understandable that you felt the way you did about everything. You've lost an important person in your life. You just needed to be reminded that life goes on and your grandmother wouldn't want anything less for you."

Tears came to Quinn's eyes as she looked at the two men and just nodded her head knowingly. All she could muster was a simple, quiet, "Well, thank you."

"Okay, enough of this emotional bullshit, let's get packed up and hit the road before it gets too late and snows much more. I don't have fucking boots to wear and my shoes are going to get ruined." François was sounding much more awake now that he had eaten.

"Oh my God! I'll loan you my grandfather's boots to save your precious Italian leather shoes." Quinn mocked.

TWENTY SEVEN

*D*riving home, Quinn smiled at how much François and Darcy cared for her, how much she cared for them. She was actually shocked at how her feelings for Darcy had changed.

It was getting dark outside and the snow was delaying the drive home. She knew that once she arrived home she would need to deal with the endless messages that would surely have been left by her family. The last thing she wanted was to deal with any of them but she felt stronger than she had before she went to the cabin and knew that she was ready for whatever they dished out to her.

Opening the door to her condo, she felt relieved to be home. It had been emotionally exhausting being at the cabin, and as much as she had needed to go, she was certainly more than ready to be home. Throwing her purse and keys on the hall table, she hung her coat up in the closet, headed straight to the living room and sat down. Looking at her answering machine, she cringed. There were thirty-two messages awaiting her.

"No doubt most of them will be from mother."

Reluctantly hitting the button, she listened.

"Quinn, it's your mother calling…" *No kidding.*

"…I want you to call me back, immediately. There are a few things your father and I would like to discuss with you." Delete.

"Quinn, it's your mother calling…" Rolling her eyes, Quinn listened.

155

"Why haven't you called me back? I left you a message yesterday. There's no need to be rude. Call me immediately." Delete.

And so it went on. There were a few messages from Darcy and the majority from her mother. As the messages continued she could tell her mother had become more and more agitated.

"This is completely unacceptable…" Delete.

And then, "How dare you ignore me this way. I won't stand for it." Delete.

Another message was clearly less amicable. "That queer French friend of yours is no bloody help at all. He claims not to know where you are. I'm sure that's complete and utter bulls…nonsense. I highly recommend you call me." Delete.

Eventually, her mother, not having heard from her eldest daughter, clearly dragged Quinn's father into things. He had left a couple of messages for her.

"Quinn, this is your father calling. This behaviour of yours is completely unacceptable. I will not stand for you ignoring your mother the way you have been…" *Oh my God.* "I demand you call us, immediately!" *Clearly that didn't happen.*

The very last message was her mother. "Quinn, you always were an intolerable child. Perhaps one day you will finally grow up like your sister. God knows I've had enough of this ridiculous attitude of yours…" and so the message went on. Quinn deleted it before it was complete. *My God, Mother. You are a raving lunatic.*

Deleting the last of the messages, Quinn was tired and decided to go to bed. She had no intention of calling her parents tonight but relented at the fact that she needed to do so in the morning. Putting the food away and throwing away the now dead roses Darcy had sent her before going to the cabin, she quickly changed and crawled into bed, almost instantaneously falling asleep.

Waking to the sound of the phone ringing, Quinn hesitated to pick it up for fear it was one of her parents but figured she might just as well 'face the music' as they say. Looking at her phone, she was relieved to see it wasn't her mother nor her father.

Still groggy from sleep, she answered, "Hello?"

"Quinn! Do meet me at Dills and Dolls! I can't go another day without a latte."

"Oh my God, François! Don't be so damn perky sounding."

"C'mon, get your ass out of bed and meet me in an hour at Dills and Dolls. After spending so much time in the middle of nowhere, I need a good latte and a noisy crowded city." François sounded desperate.

"You are so melodramatic, François. You were at the cabin for all of one night." Quinn laughed and shook her head in amazement at her friend's over dramatization.

"See you in an hour, Sweetheart."

Hanging up the phone, Quinn quickly got out of bed, showered, dressed and headed to Dills and Dolls. Arriving, she immediately looked around to see if Sasha was there. Not seeing her, Quinn headed over to sit down opposite her friend.

"Really? Was it really all that bad?"

"Yes! I'm desperate for a latte, I tell you. A good latte, Q. They have servers here now."

"Really?" Shaking her head Quinn caught the eye of Jorge, one of the regular baristas, who immediately came to the table.

"Hey, Quinn. Where have you been? I haven't seen you here for a bit."

Quinn noticed that Jorge never looked at her as he spoke, only at François.

"Jorge, my handsome friend. You really must bring me a latte. I'm desperate."

"Of course, François."

Is that blushing I'm seeing? Does Jorge have a thing for François? Quinn became very curious. This was something she never really noticed before but was going to pay much more attention to in the future.

"I'll have the same, thanks." Realizing Jorge hadn't heard a word she said, Quinn tried once more. "Jorge, I'll have a chai tea latte, please." He was completely distracted by François. Clearing her throat Quinn spoke louder this time. "Jorge!"

"Oh yes, sorry, Quinn. What was that you wanted, a latte?"

"Yes, the usual, a chai tea latte, please." Quinn smirked as she spoke.

"Sure, no problem. Be right back." And with that, Jorge was off.

"Did you see that?"

"See what?" François looked around to see what he was missing.

"Did you see how Jorge looked at you?"

"What do you mean how he looked at me?" François acted confused but began to blush.

"Oh, no! Really? You two?" Quinn asked.

"Well…" Hesitating, François fessed up. "Yes, us two, and I don't want to hear a thing about it. Do you understand?" François' defences were up. He knew how much Quinn liked to tease him.

"Wow! I'm shocked really."

"Why? Why would you be shocked, Q? What's wrong with me dating Jorge? He's a great guy, handsome and actually quite funny. He's wonderful."

"Only that he's dating someone else. Have you not learned your lesson?" She was surprised François would again date someone who was already in a relationship.

"Ah, but you're wrong. Jorge and Stan broke up a few months ago. It was only recently that I found this out."

Relieved, Quinn asked, "How many times have you gone out?" She was more curious than ever now.

"Just a few dates and he's a wonderful guy. He loves fashion. We have a lot in common…"

Chapter TWENTY SEVEN

François stopped speaking as he watched Jorge approach their table.

"Here are your lattes and if there is anything else, please just let me know." Jorge smiled at Quinn but lingered as he gazed at François. Walking away, he even looked back over his shoulder in François' direction.

Noticing François staring in return, Quinn smiled, happy for her friend. He needed someone stable in his life and from what she knew of Jorge, he was very grounded and just an all round great guy. *Let's hope it lasts more than a few weeks, unlike all his other relationships.* She knew she was being cynical and quite frankly hypocritical but she was still hopeful.

"Have you spoken to your parents yet?" François asked. "God knows I've heard from your mother more in the last couple of weeks than I have since I met you. She's a huge pain in the...." Stopping, he realized he should be careful about what he says.

"Go ahead! Say it! She's a huge pain in the ass. I know it and no I haven't called them. I honestly have nothing to say to them, François. What the hell do I say when they tell me I must sell the cabin. They won't listen to me and they know very well I don't have the money to fix the place up. My God, my father was lining up a real estate agent for me!"

François cut in, "You wouldn't consider borrowing money from them, would you?"

"Oh good God, no! There is no way in hell I would borrow a penny from them and my grandmother didn't want me to either." Quinn realized that her reaction was a bit overdramatic. "I'm just unsure of what I should do."

"Your mother told me that she wanted to meet up with you to discuss your..." Using two fingers on each hand, François made imaginary quote signs as he spoke, "options." Putting his hands back down, he rolled his eyes and added, "...whatever the hell that means."

"I suppose I should call them but it's just too nerve-wracking. I think they've all lost their God-damned minds."

"How you deal with them, I will never know. If she wasn't such a good client I would tell her exactly what I think." Looking across the room, François watched Jorge as he worked.

Quinn noticed a small smile appear. Ignoring it, she answered. "There are days I'm not sure either." Thinking for a few minutes she added, "I'll give mother a call this afternoon and see what she has to say."

"Have you thought of meeting up with her and taking Darcy along with you when you do? She will have to behave herself with him there. Might take the pressure off you. Maybe even knowing you have a serious boyfriend might get her off your back."

"Really? Do you even know me at all?"

"What?!"

"Are you crazy? I'm not taking Darcy to meet up with my mother and I sure as hell won't tell her about him. First of all, I can handle this myself and secondly, I wouldn't want to subject him to the nightmare. He already knows too much. I'm surprised he hasn't run for the hills. I would rather not scare him off before our relationship even gets started."

Smiling, François gave Quinn a knowing look. "So, you plan on this relationship lasting, do you?"

Giving her friend a dry look, Quinn scolded herself for mistakenly letting her feelings be known.

"Okay. Okay. You never thought you would hear me say something like that about a man."

"I'm not saying a word..." Laughing, François continued. "It's so true about your mother though. She could drive anyone away within minutes of meeting her," he lamented. "I have no idea why *I'm* still hanging around with you," he teased.

"Oh, thanks a lot!" Quinn frowned.

"That woman has bigger balls than I do! I should have scurried off in shame long ago."

They both laughed knowing this to be true.

TWENTY EIGHT

*B*ack home again, Quinn returned her mother's calls.

"Hello, Mother, it's Quinn. You called?" *Repeatedly for days.*

"So glad you finally decided to call your mother, Quinn. What was so important that you couldn't return my call for over two weeks?" *Everything.*

"What do you want, Mother?" Quinn responded very coolly.

Hearing a frustrated sigh at the other end of the phone, Quinn waited for a response.

"Quinn, your father and I wanted to speak to you about..." Hesitating for a moment, her mother continued, "...about your grandmother's cabin."

"*My* cabin and we have nothing to speak about, Mother." Quinn was firm in her reply.

"Well, your father and I think we do."

"The fact of the matter is, the cabin belongs to me. I will do as I wish with it. You have no input and regardless of what you say or do, I will be keeping it, so you might just as well forget talking to me about it."

"Quinn, you are so exasperating! Why won't you listen to reason? We have discussed it as a family..."

"As a family? As a family, Mother? For God's sake, you have no right to 'discuss it as a family' because I own the cabin and I am the one who makes the decisions about it! Who the hell do you think you are?!"

"Quinn, now settle down this instant. I refuse to argue with you. You know as well as I do that your grandparents bought that…that… Godforsaken cabin on a ridiculous whim. They never did have sound judgement and they certainly never spent their money wisely, not to mention, why in the name of God would they ever think that buying an old run-down cabin would be a good idea in any respect?"

"Mother, I think you should stop." Quinn was getting angrier with every word her mother spoke. She especially hated her mother criticizing her grandparents.

"It's the truth, Quinn. Your father and I advised against it. We wanted them to buy a beautiful home near us that wouldn't have been such a 'money-pit'. But no, they refused, saying they were following their dream." With forced laughter she continued, "Such as it was. When your grandfather died, your grandmother wouldn't even consider leaving that horrible place. I insisted she not live there on her own but oh, no, your grandmother's stubborn streak set in and she absolutely refused to come live with your father and me at the time. Honestly! That woman…you're just like her, Quinn. You have her stubborn trait and quite frankly neither one of you ever had any common sense whatsoever…"

Quinn grew so angry that she became surprisingly calm when she spoke.

"Mother, you need to understand something. Once Grandma's ashes are ready for spreading around the property, I will allow you, Father, Madison and Bradley to come to my property to spread them and then you will never be allowed to set foot on that property again. I do not want, nor will I ever want, a penny from you. I'm tired of your snootiness, I'm tired of being judged by all of you and I'm tired of having to almost beg forgiveness for my lifestyle choices. I don't care that you disapprove. I really don't care what you have to say about me but don't you dare say anything to the contrary about *my* grandparents!"

"You seem to forget that they were *my* parents, Quinn, and that I am the matriarch of this family now and I deserve the respect that comes with that. You would do well to remember this."

"Mother, you can call yourself whatever you like, it doesn't make it so." Quinn stated.

"Listen here, Quinn Esther Fairchild! I am still your mother and I demand respect." Her mother spoke firmly at the other end of the phone.

"That's laughable!"

"What do you mean by that?" her mother questioned.

"You may say that, but you never seemed to remember that when it came to your own mother. You disrespected her all the time. You never once took into consideration what she wanted, what they wanted. You only thought of yourself and how it would look down at the club. You didn't care that they bought the cabin because it was best for them. You only cared what your snooty friends would think and how it would look if people found out that your parents lived in a small, old, run-down cabin out in the middle of nowhere. You made your feelings quite clear. So don't you dare talk to me about respect."

"You are a very hurtful child, Quinn. Your father and I raised you better than this."

"Oh my God! You always manage to make it perfectly clear that I am a disappointment but you know what's different now, Mother? The difference is that I've finally managed to figure out that the problem isn't me, after all. No, the problem is all of you. I've got a renewed attitude and as far as I'm concerned, you and Father can take your money and your attitudes and shove them up your snooty little asses!" Quinn's voice grew louder as she spoke although her body was shaking.

"How dare you speak to me that way, Quinn!" The sound of shock resonated in her mother's voice as she replied.

Quinn calmly finished up. "Good-bye, Mother and don't bother calling François about me. He is no longer your lifeline to me."

Quinn smiled as she heard her mother say, "You wretched child...", as she was hanging up the phone.

Quinn couldn't stop shaking and was somewhat confused by how she felt at this particular moment. *Am I relieved? Sad? Angry? I have no idea.*

Sitting for a moment, she fully expected her mother to call her back immediately and give Quinn a piece of her mind, however, the phone never rang. She was relieved. She needed time to process the conversation that had just taken place.

"I need a drink." Getting up, Quinn opened the fridge, pulled out a bottle of wine and poured herself a glass. Taking a couple of big gulps, she refilled her glass, then grabbed the bottle in her other hand and went to sit back down in the living room. She was still shaking but was calming down with every sip of wine she took.

"Oh my God! I think I may have disowned my family." She surprisingly felt relieved, yet terrified.

Startled by her mobile ringing, Quinn saw that it was François and quickly picked it up.

"François, you will never believe what just happened."

"Do tell, Q." He was anxious to hear. "I love nothing more than drama when it isn't my own."

After explaining what had just taken place with her mother, Quinn nervously laughed hearing François' reaction.

"Get the fuck out! You rock! It's about fucking time you told your mother off, Q! And you even told her to stay away from me too! Oh my God, thank you…I am so grateful!" Suddenly stopping, François grew concerned.

"No! Wait! You didn't tell her to stop buying clothes from me, did you? She's one of our best clients!"

"Oh my God, François, are you kidding me?"

"Okay, okay. Fine! I'm legit proud of you. It's about time you stood up for yourself with them. They are so…overbearing. How do you feel right now?"

"I'm not sure how I feel. I think I feel great but I can't stop shaking."

"I would have loved to be a fly on the wall. That must have been some heated conversation."

Pondering for a moment, François anxiously asked, "But, honestly, Q, do you think your mother will stop coming to our shop?"

"François!"

"Alright! Okay..." François was reluctant to let the question go unanswered but knew enough not to press the issue.

"You know, François, I've spent decades being ordered around by my family. I've been miserable the entire time and it takes the death of my grandmother to get me to finally speak up for myself."

"Did you really tell your mother to shove their money and attitude up their asses?" François knew she had but wanted to hear it again.

"Yup, I sure as hell did!" Quinn and François laughed out loud together but the more Quinn spoke of the conversation she had with her mother, the more she grew anxious. She slowly stopped laughing as the reality of what occurred began to hit her.

"Oh my God, François! I just disowned my family! I just told my mother to shove things up her ass. Oh my God! What have I done?" She began to pace the floor. Panic slowly set in.

"You did the right thing, Q. It was long overdue." Her friend reassured her.

"No, I shouldn't have done that. I need to call my mother back and apologize." She felt like she might hyperventilate, she couldn't stop pacing and her breathing was very rapid.

"The hell you are! Quinn, get your shit together, girl." François urged his friend to calm down.

"I have to! I'll have to call and apologize. I'll have no family, no nothing. What the hell am I going to do?" Quinn was panicked. "I mean, it was so stupid of me. So fucking typical! How could I speak to my mother like that? What kind of daughter does that? What is wrong with me?"

"Quinn, relax."

"No, I shouldn't have done that, François. I should never have lost my temper like that."

She was having trouble thinking straight, her mind was racing and she was frantically trying to figure out how to repair the damage she had caused.

"Quinn!" François raised his voice loud enough so he could be heard over Quinn's ranting.

"What?!" She was drawn to attention.

"Just calm the fuck down!" He knew that he needed to shake his friend out of her momentary state of panic.

"Why are you yelling at me like that? I can hear you, you know." She became annoyed.

"You need to get a fucking grip. You need to realize that there was nothing wrong with what you did! Stop being so melodramatic, that's *my* job. Get it together, girl, and don't you dare call your mother back. This was a long time coming. It's just about time you said what needed to be said so just take a deep breath and relax. Do you honestly think your parents will disown you?"

"Yes! Yes I do!" she answered immediately.

"They won't disown you because they are fucking control freaks, Q. They need to know what's going on in your life. They don't have it in them…well, your mother doesn't have it in her…to walk away. So, just take a deep breath and realize that what you did was necessary. It was about time you defended yourself."

Thinking for a moment, Quinn started to calm down.

"I suppose you could be right. It's just that I have never spoken to my mother that way before."

"I *am* right and what you actually mean is that you've never told her to shove something up her ass before." François laughed.

"Stop laughing! I'm serious."

"I know you are, as am I. Relax, have a glass of wine…"

"I've almost finished a whole damn bottle!"

"Right then, well, have you at least calmed down enough that I don't have to worry that you will call back and try to make nice?" François needed assurance.

"Yes, yes, I suppose so. I have no idea what I would say anyway. 'Hello, Mother, I'm sorry I told you to shove pretty much everything up your snooty little asses. No I don't think that will help. I'm sure my father will be picking her up off the floor about now and giving her some meds to calm her nerves."

Laughing, François needed to ask, "But, seriously, Q, do you think your mother will stop buying clothes from me?" François knew the repercussions would be immense if that occurred.

"François! Stop about the damn clothes."

"Alright, okay, I'm sure she won't." He wasn't convinced.

"Listen, must go. Fayeed's new model has started this morning and we need to rework everything to fit her. It has set us back weeks but thankfully we should still be ready before the spring show. Did you want to join Jorge and me for dinner tonight?"

"No, thanks anyway. Darcy is coming by tonight and bringing in dinner for us. You two lovebirds go and have a good time."

"Will do. Your loss."

Quinn laughed to herself as she said good-bye. Her friend was nothing less than interesting.

TWENTY NINE

That evening, Darcy arrived with Chinese food in hand and a bottle of wine. Quinn couldn't have been more grateful than she was at that moment for a distraction.

"I knew you wouldn't have much food in the house and I must say there is no better way to spend a Saturday night than over Chinese food and a bottle of red wine," Darcy announced as he finished placing everything out on the kitchen counter.

Walking into the kitchen, Quinn smiled at the sight of the food before her.

"Are those chicken balls? I love chicken balls!" Quinn was almost drooling and immediately reached for them.

Grabbing their food and heading to the living room, Darcy looked at Quinn knowing that something wasn't quite right.

"Everything okay, Quinn? You don't seem your usual sarcastic, outgoing self," Darcy joked.

Quinn shook her head and explained the conversation that had taken place with her mother.

"I'm sure my parents are right about the fact that I should sell the cabin. It really will cost a fortune to fix up but I just can't bring myself to do it. I love it there and my grandparents loved it there. My grandmother left it to me, confident that I wouldn't sell it. How could I betray her like that?"

"Quinn, you know I could help you with it."

"No, but thanks anyway, Darcy. I just don't have the money. I'm sure I will figure something out." She had a hard time convincing herself of that, let alone Darcy.

Thinking for a moment, Darcy offered. "No worries, I could loan you the money just to get you started."

"Why would you do that?" Quinn quickly grew defensive. "You hardly know me."

"Because I can, and I want to help you." Darcy reasoned.

"Really, Darcy. I appreciate the offer but, no, thank you." Quinn wasn't about to drag Darcy into her problems. It was just about time she grew up and took care of this herself. *I don't want to let Grandma down. I need to do this myself.*

"C'mon Quinn. What's wrong with me helping you?"

"I have to be able to do this on my own."

"No, you don't. Just let me help you." Darcy implored.

It had been an emotional day and Quinn's patience was worn thin. She was desperately trying not to lose her temper. She knew he was being kind to her but she needed time to think things through.

"We could have that cabin whipped into shape in no time. I would have to assess it to see exactly where the problems are and establish what to do first but that wouldn't take long. We could start now or in the spring..."

Quinn tuned him out as he spoke. *Why won't he just leave me alone to deal with this? My God! I wish he would just shut the hell up! You're right Mom and Dad, I really am a loser. I'm sick to death of never measuring up. I sometimes wonder if I really can survive without you. I hate this! I hate all of it! Well, I'll show you! I'll do this and I don't need anyone to do it for me.*

"...I think it would be pretty exciting to be able to help you with it..." Darcy continued.

Chapter TWENTY NINE

"Oh my God, would you please stop! My parents never thought I could survive out on my own without their help, without their money and I have. Well, sort of…and I have no intention of proving to them otherwise. I can do this and I will! I refuse to be the loser daughter that they always assumed me to be." She was adamant. "I don't need their help, Darcy, and I sure as hell don't need yours. I don't need anyone's help. I can do this on my own. The last thing I need is charity…."

"I know you don't need charity and this isn't charity."

"Yes it is and no, I won't let you."

"Okay…would it make you feel any better if I charged you for it?" Darcy joked.

"What?! You mean to tell me that you want to help me but now you want to charge me for it? How is *that* helping me? That's the most ridiculous thing I've ever heard!" Quinn couldn't believe what she was hearing. "Nice." Sarcasm practically dripped off the word as she said it.

"What do you want from me? I'm trying to help you." Darcy was getting frustrated with her attitude.

"I don't want anything from you! That's the whole point! That's what you aren't getting."

"Why are you being so pigheaded about this? I'm your boyfriend and I want to help you." Darcy again tried to reason with her.

"I am *not* being pigheaded, I don't need your help…" she shouted in defiance unable to control what was coming out of her mouth. The frustration of the day was coming to a head. "…and I sure as hell don't need a rich man's charity!"

The silence in the room was palpable.

Darcy nodded his head slightly with understanding but said nothing. Walking to the front door he grabbed his coat, picked up his wallet, put it in his pants pocket, then picked up his keys. Opening the door, he turned back and looked at Quinn who followed him, confused by what was happening.

"Quinn, one day you will realize that doing it all on your own in life isn't necessarily a sign of strength and independence, sometimes it's just…alone." And with that, Darcy left, closing the door behind him, leaving Quinn stunned by the unexpected turn of events.

Tears coming to her eyes, Quinn knew that she had completely over reacted. She knew she hadn't meant what she said to Darcy and regretted every last hurtful word but wasn't sure what to do about it now.

THIRTY

"What the hell is so important that I had to end a perfectly awesome dinner date with Jorge to come see you?" François was out of breath as he stormed through the door of Quinn's condo and into her living room. Stopping cold, he was shocked at the sight before him.

"What the..."

Quinn was curled up on the couch, dressed in her pajamas and cardigan, wearing her old pair of bunny slippers that François had given her for her birthday as a joke years prior. There she was, tissue in her hand, nose red from blowing it, eyes red and swollen from crying.

"What the hell? Where's Darcy? What's going on?" François was confused.

Quinn blew her nose loudly and tossed the tissue onto the end table where François noticed a big pile already strewn across it, with some even on the floor below. Walking over, he sat down on the couch facing Quinn.

"Q?"

Between tears, Quinn updated François on the events of the evening. François sat silently contemplating what to say.

"François? What should I do? Everything is a disaster these days. Nothing's gone right since my grandmother died." Quinn sobbed through her words. She was looking for the consolation her friend always provided when she was upset. She needed it now more than ever.

Quinn curiously looked at her friend, unsure of why he wasn't speaking. Saying nothing, François got up, went into the kitchen and returned moments later with a glass of water. Quinn wondered what he was doing when he suddenly threw the water in her face.

"What the fuck, François!? What's that all about?" Quinn was shocked. Spitting water out of her mouth, she wiped her eyes and face but before she could say anything more, her friend suddenly exploded.

"What the hell is wrong with you?! Have you lost your fucking mind?!"

Quinn was stunned.

"Do you always have to speak before you think? Maybe, just maybe, for once, you could keep your damn mouth shut, get that chip off your shoulder and not be so fucking defensive all the time!" He knew his friend needed a shake up and now was the time to give it to her.

Shocked by what François was saying, Quinn stopped crying and sat staring at him. She wasn't sure what was happening. She couldn't remember a time he had been more angry with her than he was at that very moment and he clearly wasn't holding anything back.

"Have you not figured out by now that Darcy is nothing like your family? Have you not figured out by now that he's crazy about you and I might add, you're crazy about him? You're just too damn self-absorbed to even recognize that this man genuinely cares about you and wants to help you. Not because you are a charity case and sure as hell not because you're the most likeable person in the world, God knows that's not the case. No, this man actually wants to help you because he cares about you! He's out of his mind, in my humble opinion, because the way you have behaved, you don't deserve the help! If it were me, I would let you cry your snotty-nosed self into oblivion and walk away. You'll be lucky if he ever forgives you after the 'wife' situation and now after this ridiculous tirade today."

"How dare you?" Quinn was incensed by what her friend was saying.

"How dare *I*?! How dare *you?* How dare *you* think you are the only person in this world who has mommy and daddy issues. How dare *you* think that you need to have a lifetime pity party because Spencer cheated on you? How dare *you* treat people the way you have been just because you can't get past one asshole and his cheating ways? Get a grip, Q! Shake it off and pull yourself together!"

Quinn sat silently staring at her friend before her, listening to him spewing everything he felt she needed to hear.

"Quinn, you know I love you but I'm sick to death of watching you treat yourself like shit. Quite frankly, you shouldn't be treating any of those guys you've been with like shit either or you're just as bad as Spencer, but I don't care about them, I care about you. You've been on a path of self-pity since you left Spencer and it's time to get off the damn pity train and get on with things. You are so fucking blinded by what happened with Spencer and with your parents that you can't even see that Darcy actually gives a shit about you."

Thinking for a moment, he continued, "I'm tired of watching you do this. Get the fuck on with your life, Q!"

Quinn was hurt knowing that François had reached his limit with her. It hurt her to hear what he had to say. He was her only other champion and she felt more alone at this very moment than she ever had. Although she wasn't sure if she was more hurt, or angry by it all, she did realize that her friendship with him was far more important to her than the failed relationship with her parents. She wasn't sure what she would ever do without François' friendship if he walked out of her life right now. One thing she did know, though, was that he was right about everything. As much as she had avoided facing the truth, clearly François felt it was time to verbally 'slap her in the face' with it and all she could do was sit in stunned silence listening to him force her to face the truth.

"Now, I think it's just about time you pull yourself together and do what you have to do to get your life back on track. It's time to be happy and it's time to realize that not every guy is like Spencer. You sure as hell don't need to be so fucking cynical all the time and you sure as hell don't need to prove to anyone that you can make it on your own. For God's sake, this is exhausting for *me*. I can't imagine what it's like for *you*, always with a chip on your shoulder, always putting on a show of defiance. It must drain every ounce of energy from you. Quite frankly, you've become quite jaded and blinded by it all. Move on, Quinn. It's time. Swallow your pride, go find Darcy, have passionate sex with him and give us all a bloody break."

Not waiting for his friend to respond, François walked over, gave her a kiss on the forehead.

"I love you, Quinn. Now go find the other person who loves you and beg, grovel, apologize...whatever the fuck it takes to make amends with him."

Watching François leave, Quinn felt numb by all he said. She did know much of what he said was true. It was like a stab to the heart to hear it but she knew he was right. Soon she was, once again, sobbing uncontrollably. It seemed to be all she knew how to do lately.

THIRTY ONE

aking with a start, Quinn felt stiff all over, confused by where she was. Opening her eyes she realized that she had fallen asleep on the couch on her stomach with her head turned to one side. Rolling over onto her back, she flinched, feeling a kink in her neck. Lying there for a few minutes, she thought back to the night before and felt embarrassed by her behaviour with Darcy.

Oh my God! How could I have been so stupid? Putting her hands over her face, Quinn moaned out loud.

Sitting up, she looked around at the mess of her living room. Used Kleenex all over the floor and end table; her plate of half eaten food. Then she noticed the second plate of food sitting there and Darcy's glass of wine on the other end table.

"What the hell have I done?" Things seemed so much clearer than they had the night before…or ever. Her friend had single-handedly managed to clear the fog out of her head that had been sitting there for years. He gave her much to think about…too much. Lying there deep in thought, she knew what she had to do.

Grabbing her mobile, Quinn dialled Darcy's number and reached his voicemail. Hanging up, she tried calling François. No answer. *Can I blame either of them?*

Getting up she grabbed her purse and left.

Pulling up in front of the Monaghan's Outdoor World office building, Quinn was nervous. She knew she had to go in but wasn't sure how she would be received. Most likely not well but she had to try. Sitting for a few moments she nervously wrapped hair around her index finger trying to gather the nerve to open the car door and move. It was lunchtime and many people were coming and going in and out of the building. It was a dull, overcast day, lightly snowing with most everyone appearing to be wearing business clothing and overcoats, others in more casual coats wearing jeans and work boots.

Suddenly getting cold feet, Quinn decided to leave. *I really don't think I can take another person 'enlightening' me on just how foolish I have been lately. He probably hates me anyway.* She was convinced she couldn't face Darcy, not yet, but just as she was about to leave, she saw him walk out of the building dressed in a business suit, overcoat unbuttoned and open.

Watching as he walked across the courtyard, Quinn felt even more humiliated by her behaviour the night before. *I can't do this. I better go before he sees me.*

Hearing the car start, Darcy looked up in her direction. For a moment, Quinn thought he was going to ignore her and continue on his way. She wouldn't have blamed him if he had but to her surprise he started making his way towards her. That's when panic set in.

Oh shit! I'm not ready for this. Fussing with her hair, Quinn took in a deep breath knowing she had no other choice but to face him.

Turning the car off, she opened the door. Stepping out, she stood awkwardly beside the car. Self-consciously smiling at him she wrapped her sweater tighter trying to fend off the cold. Looking down at the sidewalk she felt completely embarrassed and wondered what he must think of her.

"Quinn?" Darcy approached her with a puzzled look on his face.

Biting down on her lower lip, Quinn wasn't sure what to say at first.

"Why are you here?" he asked.

Thinking for a moment she felt tears come to her eyes.

"Darcy...I'm..." She was choking on her words. "...I'm so sorry."

Chapter THIRTY ONE

When he said nothing, she continued.

"I owe you an apology. You absolutely didn't deserve how I treated you. I was completely..."

"Unreasonable," he interjected matter-of-factly.

Looking surprised, she conceded, "Yes. I was unreasonable."

"And short-tempered," he added without hesitation.

Narrowing her eyes, she once again agreed, "Yes. And short-tempered."

"And short-sighted," he continued.

Becoming annoyed, she reluctantly acknowledged, "And short-sighted."

"And unfair."

"O...kaaayyy...and unfair." She tried to contain her sarcasm as she spoke.

"Oh, and don't forget...and this is my personal favourite...completely irrational." Darcy grinned as he emphasized the word 'irrational', knowing very well that he was pushing her buttons.

Gritting her teeth, she tried to control her temper. "Well, maybe not *completely* irrational."

"Oh, I would definitely say that you were completely irrational." Darcy insisted.

The annoyed look on her face brought a smile to Darcy's. He wasn't about to let her off the hook too easily. She deserved to squirm.

Changing the subject, he asked, "Is there a reason why you're here to see me in your pajamas...and are they..."

Lifting her left pajama bottom leg to get a better look, he continued, "Yup, I was right, they are bunny slippers."

Surprised, she quickly looked down, mortified to see that, she had in fact, left home wearing her pajamas and bunny slippers. The slippers were worn from use with one ear missing from the left slipper and the right bearing a large hole where her big toe now peeked through. She had never really paid too much attention to the state they were in before now. Quickly removing them, she opened the car door and threw them inside.

Bending over to look in her side view mirror, Quinn was even more mortified to see her hair was a disastrous matted mess, her eyes puffy with mascara smudged underneath them. "Oh my God!" Licking her fingers, she wiped away as much mascara as possible before finally giving up.

Although she was annoyed at the thought of Darcy mocking her, she also knew she couldn't say anything because she had no ground to stand on after her behaviour the night before.

Deciding she had no choice but to 'own the look', Quinn swiped hair from her eyes, crossed her arms, and even though she felt completely humiliated, she still held her head high waiting for Darcy to say something in response to her apology.

"Rough night?" he teased.

"You think?" she responded abruptly.

Sighing, she knew she had to make amends. "Listen, Darcy, I really…"

"I know. You're sorry for being a complete ass and you don't know how you can ever make it up to me for being so irrational and defensive…"

"Oh my God! Why do you have to be so damn frustrating all the time?" She was starting to lose her temper again.

"But that's part of my charm." He grinned.

"Really? *That's* your charm?" She couldn't help the sarcasm.

"So, you were saying?" Darcy waited for her to continue, knowing that he was completely disrupting her moment.

"Um…" She had lost her train of thought. "I honestly can't remember…"

"Oh, I remember. You were apologizing to me." Darcy reminded her.

Giving him a dirty look, Quinn gathered her thoughts.

"Right. Okay. I'm so sorry for the way I acted last night. It was…"

Laughing, Darcy said, "I'm sorry but I just can't take you seriously while you are wearing pajamas, knowing that you are freezing your ass off standing there in sock feet while those bunny slippers are wasting away in the backseat of your car."

She had to admit, her feet were freezing on the wet ground and as much as she was trying to ignore the fact, as soon as Darcy mentioned it, she realized she needed to get warm. She wanted to finish what she had come there to say but was starting to shiver from the cold temperatures of the day.

"Oh my God, Darcy! I'm trying desperately to apologize to you for my abhorrent behaviour last night and you keep interrupting me! I am sleep deprived, I have puffy eyes from crying all night, smudged mascara, messy hair and I'm standing downtown during lunch hour in my pajamas and bloody..."

"You look quite sexy, by the way." Darcy teased.

In utter disbelief, Quinn continued, "...bunny slippers, trying to beg your forgiveness. It was uncalled for and I'm sorry. You didn't deserve to be treated that way."

Thinking for a moment, Darcy responded, "It's true. I didn't deserve it and I forgive you. Now, do you feel like some lunch?"

"What?" Quinn was puzzled. "That's it?"

Contemplating her question, Darcy answered, "Yup. That's it."

"You're not angry? Not going to yell at me and tell me that you never want to see me again?" Quinn was noticeably shivering from the cold now.

Once again contemplating her question, Darcy said, "Ah, nope."

"But I deserve to be told off."

"Yup."

"So, why aren't you giving me a piece of your mind, then? Why aren't you yelling at me?" Quinn was dumbfounded.

"Why?"

"Yes, why? Why aren't you yelling at me?" Her curiosity was piqued not to mention she was quite confused by his response.

"Well, I figure you have suffered enough humiliation by standing here, freezing in the cold and looking like…" He used his eyes to look her up and down. "…like *this*, that there is nothing more that needs to be said."

"Oh," was all Quinn could say.

"Now, can you please get back in your car, put the damn bunny slippers back on and crank the heat so you stop shivering? I'm cold just looking at you. Why in hell didn't you wear a coat? It's freezing outside."

Before she could answer, he said, "Let me take you home so you can…" Thinking on his words, Darcy finished, "…do something with yourself."

Directing Quinn to get into the passenger's side, Darcy slid in behind the wheel and turned the car on.

"Oh, very nice. Thank you. I suppose that was your so-called charm, again."

"It's a gift."

With the heat up high it wasn't long before the car and Quinn began to warm up. She had to admit she couldn't believe she had left the house dressed the way she was. She had clearly been in worse shape than she realized.

THIRTY TWO

*O*nce home, Quinn quickly had a hot shower and got dressed into warm clothes. She was beginning to feel better…like the weight of the world had been lifted off her shoulders.

Walking out of her bedroom, she immediately smelled the aroma of fresh made coffee and smiled. In the kitchen, she found Darcy doing the dishes.

"So, it's cheese omelettes and toast for lunch since all that Chinese food had to be thrown out because it sat out on the counter all night long, not to mention, your fridge is almost bare, other than the little bit of food you brought home from the cabin."

She couldn't tell if Darcy was scolding her, teasing her, or a bit of both.

Looking up at Quinn, Darcy offered, "It's okay though, because I had a hankering for an omelette and, well, you're quite lucky because I happen to be the best omelette maker around."

"Is that so?" Quinn grinned as she watched him crack eggs into a bowl.

"Absolutely. I was taught at a very young age all about the art of making a good omelette, so you just sit back and watch the master at work."

Quinn laughed. She was enjoying how comfortable Darcy made her feel. She was learning to accept his unconditional friendship and love. Quinn could tell she had lost the battle with her heart. He had grown on her. Her heart had even fluttered at the sight of him as she walked into the kitchen. *I am definitely falling in love with this guy.*

"Quinn? Hello?"

Shaking herself back to the moment, "I'm sorry, what were you saying?"

"One piece of toast or two? With butter or without?" Darcy stood holding two pieces of bread over the toaster.

"Two please," she smiled. "With butter."

"Two, with butter, it is!" Popping the toaster down, Darcy went back to finishing the omelettes, which Quinn had to admit were looking rather professionally done.

• ● •

"I must confess. That was the best cheese and veggie omelette I have ever eaten." Quinn felt so content. She had a full stomach, she was warm and dressed in clean jeans, a sweatshirt and had cleaned up the mess in her living room. With a hot cup of coffee in her hand, she smiled. Life felt pretty damn good at this very moment, and then, the phone rang.

She let it go to message, forgetting that the volume was up and Darcy would hear who was calling. Her content, happy moment was over.

"Quinn. This is your mother calling. Your father and I have had just about enough of your irresponsible behaviour and have decided that you clearly don't have the common sense nor the proper judgement to deal with this matter of the cabin. Since you don't have a penny to your name and you obviously can't afford to keep it, we will be buying it from you. We will fix it up and sell it, making a good profit. We can have Marshall Fox from the club put it on the market. Since your father is a lawyer, he is writing up the papers today and his office will be calling you to come by to sign them. Don't be a fool..."

With that, the message cut off. *Thank God!* Quinn was completely humiliated knowing that Darcy had heard the message but she supposed now was as good a time as any for him to hear first hand what she was dealing with. If he decided not to stick around she would understand.

Chapter THIRTY TWO

The phone once again rang. Not wanting to get into it with her mother while Darcy was there, Quinn tried to reach the machine to turn the volume off but was too late. She was dreading to hear what else her mother had to say.

"Quinn, it's your mother again. Whatever you do, don't be foolish enough not to sign those papers. You always were irrational like your grandmother and quite frankly, it's unbecoming. Your father didn't work hard all his life to have his daughter living like a pauper. It's utterly humiliating for him...for us. You should have married Spencer. He had money, status...who cares about some petty affair he had. What harm would it have done to turn a blind eye...?"

Hearing her mother sigh over the phone, Quinn was tempted to pick it up to finish the conversation once and for all but couldn't bring herself to move.

"Oh never mind, just call your father and make arrangements to sign those papers. Quite frankly, it's your only way out of the poor house. God knows, I have no idea how you live the way..."

After the call ended, Quinn sat with her head down, unable to speak, feeling ashamed and wondering what Darcy would think of her now. Her heart sank. She had been an utter emotional mess since she met him and he just kept coming back. She didn't understand why. She was tired of the drama in her life and just when she felt things were going to be okay, now this. She couldn't help the feeling of degradation that enveloped her at that very moment. She couldn't even bring herself to look at him. The silence in the room was deafening. All she could hear was the ticking of the wall clock, and so, she waited for the fallout.

"So, I was thinking. What are your thoughts on working on an historical log cabin restoration?"

Quinn quickly looked up to see Darcy on his mobile phone and her eyes immediately welled up with tears.

THIRTY THREE

*D*arcy continued, "Yes, that's right. The name? Quinn Fairchild."

"Really? Is that so?" Darcy looked over at Quinn.

"Well, really no money at all." Darcy continued his conversation with the mysterious person on the other end of the line.

"I was thinking that you could do it as a write off and use it as a model home for people to go through or film it for clients to view for future restoration work. It could be great for marketing."

Quinn sat quietly listening to the one-sided conversation.

"Talk to your people about it and let me know. I think it's an opportunity that might help expand your business in a direction we have never thought of." Darcy sounded hopeful.

"Alrighty then. Let me know and if you receive confirmation, I can bring Quinn to meet with you and the team."

"Yes, I understand it could take time to get board approval and no promises."

"Great! I'll talk to you later." With that, Darcy ended his call.

"Who was that?" Quinn was curious.

"That was my sister. She is COO of a construction firm. Nothing to do with the family business. It is something she and her ex-husband, Charlie, own together and even though they are divorced they still work together and it's quite a successful little business. Charlie is the CEO."

"What's the name of it?" Quinn wanted to know more.

"Weller Construction Corp. As in Charlie Weller."

"Really? Your sister owns Weller Construction? My God, that's quite the 'little' business. It's one of the biggest construction companies around." Quinn was amazed.

"Yes, well, as I say, it's their company, together. I don't get involved with it. She sounded quite interested in the cabin restoration but needs to speak to Charlie and the board of directors about it first.

"But I don't have a penny to offer them. Why would they even consider it knowing that?" Quinn was confused.

"Because they can use it as a model home for future clientele. They've been talking about expanding the business from condos and townhouses and this just might be the niche they are looking for. Trust me, it would be a win-win situation. They aren't going to get involved in anything that won't bring in business one way or the other, I can assure you." Darcy smiled.

Thinking about it for a few minutes, Quinn reasoned with herself. *I need to take a chance. It's the only way to save the cabin so that I can keep it. Otherwise, I sell it and prove my parents right.*

"Well, what do you think?" Darcy asked.

Looking up at him, she smiled knowing that it was a terrifying risk she was nervous to take but also an opportunity she needed to take advantage of.

"What do I think?" Smiling she continued, "I think it sounds like a plan!"

THIRTY FOUR

The next day Quinn met Darcy at Dills and Dolls for a coffee.

"Have you heard from your sister?" She was excited about the possibilities.

"I did, this morning, and they are in but they need to take it to the board next month for approval to move forward. After that, it could take months to get everything in place to begin. They have never worked on historical buildings before and they need to research and see what will be involved, not to mention getting building permits." Darcy was genuinely pleased.

"Darcy, I can't thank you enough for this, and your sister. I can't believe they approved moving forward with it."

"Like I said, they've been talking about other ways of expanding their business and my sister and Charlie were more than enthusiastic about this addition to their business plan. They just need board approval and I can't see a problem with that. I can assure you, they are meticulous. Everything would be done properly."

Continuing, Darcy offered, "One thing that will need to be done is packing up the smaller items in the cabin. Everything except the larger items like furniture. That can remain."

"Okay, I can do that anytime you say." Quinn thought for a moment. "I think my grandmother would approve. My parents on the other hand won't be too happy." Quinn had to admit that she was very apprehensive about their reaction.

"Oh, I meant to tell you that your father called their office yesterday about the possibility of hiring Weller Construction to do work on the cabin before it goes up for sale."

"What?!" Quinn was amazed by the nerve of her father. "Who did he speak to?"

"Well, he left a message and after Charlie and I spoke about what was going on, Charlie returned his call last night."

"What did Charlie say to him? Quinn was curious. Her father had left several messages for her but there was no way she was going to call now until she knew how the conversation went between her father and Charlie.

"Let's just say he wasn't at all happy. Charlie told him that they were unable to take on that restoration for him since they had already been hired by the owner to work on it. When Charlie questioned his authority to request this work be done, your father just about hit the roof."

"Oh, I bet he did." Quinn chuckled. "He would be completely offended that his motives were being questioned."

Quinn didn't mention that her father had been trying to call her. She knew it was inevitable that she return his call and was admittedly nervous. Calls with her father were never comfortable. Usually she spoke with her mother. She knew it was serious business when her father wanted to speak with her.

"Well, I have to get back to work." Darcy stood as he spoke and then leaned in giving Quinn a kiss.

"Oh, and by the way, once the board approves moving forward, my sister and Charlie will need to meet up with you to have you sign papers, giving them authority to do the work on the cabin."

"Yes, of course, no problem." Quinn was genuinely excited and couldn't wait to get started.

Grabbing his jacket off the back of the chair, Darcy waved good-bye, then left.

Chapter THIRTY FOUR

Arriving home again, Quinn picked up the phone and nervously dialled her father's office.

"It's Quinn Fairchild calling, I would like to speak to my father."

Was that an irritated sigh I heard?

Momentarily, a stern voice answered the phone.

"How in hell can you afford to hire Weller Construction to restore that cabin?"

Let's cut to the chase shall we. Quinn was taken aback at how quickly her father got to the point. He was clearly frustrated.

"That's…um…well, that's really none of your business." Quinn tried to keep her voice strong.

"What the hell do you mean 'it's none of my business'? Of course it is! You know as well as I do that you don't have that kind of money, so, how the hell could you hire Weller? I can't prove it but I don't believe for one minute that they are doing any work for you."

Quinn grew angrier with every word her father screamed at her.

"What did you do? Steal the money?"

Quinn was incensed. "How dare you! That's low, even for you, Daddy!"

"I have the real estate papers all written up and I demand you get over here today to sign them, Quinn! This is all a bunch of concocted bullshit! You know it and I know it, so stop stalling and sign the God damned papers!"

Her father was clearly infuriated. Quinn remained silent until she was sure he was finished.

"Well Quinn? What have you got to say for yourself?" Her father had calmed down ever so slightly.

Thinking very carefully about how she was going to answer, Quinn was shaking with anger and nerves. He always made her feel like an incompetent child. Taking a deep breath in, she thought, *But not today.*

"I'm not signing those real estate papers, Daddy. I fully intend on restoring *my* cabin and keeping it. It's none of your business how I plan on doing it and you have no right to tell me what to do. I am not a child and I will not be intimidated by you anymore."

"How dare you speak to me that way!" Her father's authoritarian voice echoed through the phone.

"No! How dare *you* speak to *me* that way!" Quinn retorted.

"Once you left Spencer, I suspected you wouldn't add up to much of anything but you have more than surpassed my expectations. I never thought I would ever have a daughter thrown in jail after a common bar brawl, let alone one who sleeps around with every reprobate she meets, like a…"

"Like a what?" Quinn asked defiantly, curious to know what her father truly thought of her.

Hesitating for a brief moment, he added, "Like a common whore!" Almost spitting the words out through the phone he couldn't contain himself.

Now the truth comes out. His words stung.

Hearing a click at the other end of the line was her indication that the conversation was clearly over with her father. She didn't have it in her to shed another tear if she wanted to. She was angry and had cried enough recently to last a lifetime. She was fed up with allowing herself to be victimized and was finally realizing that she was no longer the same person she was when she broke up with Spencer. She had changed. The difference was, that now, she was strong, not broken.

"Fuck you, Daddy."

THIRTY FIVE

alking into Quinn's kitchen later that day, François was shocked by what he heard. "What?! No! Your father called you a fucking whore?" Sitting down, he accepted the glass of red wine Quinn offered him. "That's unbelievable!"

"Trust me, it's very believable." Quinn was still hurt by the conversation but wasn't going to falter in her decision about keeping the cabin. "I'd be lying if I said it didn't hurt or that I wasn't scared shitless but I'm tired of it all, François. Worn out and tired."

"I don't blame you, Sweetheart." François was sympathetic.

Sitting quietly sipping on wine, Quinn contemplated her next move. Exhausted by the conversation about her parents she changed the subject.

"By the way, if the board approves the decision to renovate the cabin, it needs to be emptied and you're helping me."

"Oh no! No way, Q! I am not helping you pack up that cabin and you can't make me! I already spent a night there and that was enough for me. I can't go back. I'll lose my mind and besides, I have a show to get ready for. No way, not happening!"

François panicked when Quinn notified him that he would be the one to help her pack up the cabin. Having to be there for more than a night was beyond what he could take and he was having nothing to do with it.

"Oh, you most certainly are!" Quinn was adamant. "And your show isn't till the Spring. You have plenty of time beforehand. I'm sure board approval will come sooner than later."

"Get Darcy to help you."

"Nope! You're helping me."

"Yeah, ah, no I'm not." François was intent on standing his ground. "And you can't change my mind on the matter."

"Not even for a dinner at Pier 4 for you and Jorge, my compliments?" Quinn bribed.

Stopping cold, François squinted his eyes staring at his friend.

"Really?" He asked cautiously.

"Really." Quinn confirmed.

"You aren't just saying that?" François wasn't sure whether to believe her or not.

"Nope, not just saying that." Quinn knew she had hit a chord offering Pier 4.

"Anything we want on the menu?" François inched closer to the edge of agreement.

"Anything."

"Wine and dessert included?" He wasn't going to let her off the hook too easily.

"Wine and dessert included." Quinn knew she had him hook, line and sinker now.

"But, it's nearly impossible to get reservations there. How can *you* get reservations?" François was skeptical.

"Because I have a friend who works there, that's how. Now do we have a deal or what?"

Thinking very carefully, processing everything in his mind before committing, François finally conceded.

Chapter THIRTY FIVE

"Okay, fine. It's a deal, but you better not be playing me on this, Q." François stared her down to see if she would flinch.

"I'm not playing you, François. It's a firm deal."

Thinking for a moment more, François broke out into a big smile and nodded.

"Well, alright then! It won't be easy but I'm willing to do this for you, Q…because I care."

"Yeah, right." Quinn's sarcasm was evident. "And for dinner at Pier 4."

François smiled triumphantly.

THIRTY SIX

*W*eeks had gone by. It was the Friday following New Years and Quinn was getting impatient waiting to hear of the board's approval to renovate the cabin. She was also very anxious for a meeting with Darcy's sister. She was told that the board of directors would be meeting around the holidays but there was no set date provided. She could hardly wait to hear if the board agreed to proceed. Darcy assured her that once approval was given, his sister would set a meeting with Quinn to discuss next steps.

Darcy arrived at her place for dinner and before he even took his coat off, Quinn had to ask, "Have you heard what date the board meeting is set for?"

"Actually, my sister called me before I left work. The board met last night and approved moving forward with the new business plan."

"Oh my God! That's awesome, Darcy!" Quinn was thrilled.

"My sister is going out of town next week for some retreat or something like that and would like to meet with you before she leaves."

"Sure, that's fine." Quinn was eager to start the process.

"She mentioned that she and Charlie would like to meet tomorrow morning if you are free." Darcy announced. "I know it's short notice…"

"Absolutely! What time?" Quinn's enthusiasm was evident.

"At ten o'clock. We can meet at their office." Darcy explained.

"Can't wait!" Quinn was excited.

"Where is François? I thought he was joining us for dinner?" Darcy asked.

"He is. He should be here shortly." Quinn checked the time as she spoke.

"When do you think you are going to start cleaning things out of the cabin? Not that there is any hurry. The plan isn't to start anything until late spring by the time they get everything into place. I can help you with that."

"No need. François is going to help me."

"François?!" Darcy was surprised. "You mean he is going to go back to the cabin?"

"Yup he sure is!" Quinn laughed. "He's doing it very reluctantly and certainly not without a bribe, but he's helping me."

"Only because she offered dinner for Jorge and I at Pier 4." François had walked in without being noticed. Reaching for a glass he poured himself some wine.

"Why else would I be dragging myself out to that God forsaken countryside to pack boxes?"

"You have no problem letting me pull money from my very limited savings account to pay for you and Jorge to have that ridiculously expensive dinner?" Quinn was hoping he would take pity.

"No problem, whatsoever." François said matter-of-factly.

"You are shallow, my friend." Darcy laughed.

"And proud of it." François sipped on his wine. "So what's for dinner?"

THIRTY SEVEN

*T*he next morning, Quinn put on a business suit and even a bit of make-up.

If these people are willing to foot the bill to fix up my cabin then I suppose I can put a bit of effort into getting dressed for this meeting.

Hopping into her car, Quinn put the address into her GPS and headed to the Weller Construction office. It was quite a distance out of town. Pulling up in front of the building, Quinn was surprised to see it was a rather modest brick building, mainly fronted with glass windows and only five storeys tall. On the front was the name, Weller Construction.

Walking up to the front door, Quinn stopped and looked around for Darcy before walking in. Approaching the front desk, Quinn announced herself and was directed to sit in the waiting area and told that Mrs. Weller would be there to greet her shortly.

After a few minutes, Quinn was surprised to see Darcy coming out of the elevator.

"Hi Quinn. I got here early. I was upstairs with my sister and Charlie. I said that I would come down to get you. You ready for this meeting?"

"Admittedly, I'm quite nervous."

"Well, don't be. My sister and Charlie are very approachable people. You'll like them and I have no doubt they will like you, so, let's go sign some papers."

Stepping off the elevator onto the fifth floor, Quinn was impressed to see that the floors were light coloured marble, walls painted soft grey. Immediately in front of them was an impressively large glass desk with a handsome young man sitting behind it and on the wall behind him, Weller Construction in large black modern lettering. Looking up, he smiled when he saw them.

"Mr. Monaghan, Mrs. Weller said to go right into the board room."

"Thanks, Logan."

Darcy guided Quinn around the corner to the only entrance within eyesight, an oversized, wooden double door large enough to fit a car through, in Quinn's opinion. Knocking first, Quinn could hear a male voice respond, "Come in, Darcy."

Letting Darcy walk ahead of her, Quinn saw that there was only one person sitting at the board room table. *That must be Charlie,* she speculated.

Upon seeing Quinn, the gentleman stood up and broke out into a big smile. He had short salt and pepper hair with a well groomed beard. He was shorter than Darcy and seemed to be in excellent shape. Reaching his hand out to Quinn, he introduced himself.

"You must be Quinn. I've heard so much about you. It's such a pleasure to meet you. I'm Charlie Weller."

Quinn instantly liked him. He had a warm smile and welcoming demeanour.

"Hello Charlie. It's nice to meet you as well." Quinn shook his hand and her jitters disappeared.

"Please, sit down. Darcy's sister will be here momentarily. She had an important call she needed to take. Can I offer you a coffee? Tea, perhaps?"

"Coffee would be great, thank you."

"Darcy?"

Chapter THIRTY SEVEN

"I've had enough this morning, Charlie, thanks though." Darcy pulled a chair out for Quinn and then sat down in the one beside her, their backs to the door and facing out a large window overlooking a park.

Within a few minutes, Quinn heard the door open.

"Ah, you finally made it. As you can see, Quinn is here. Let's get started shall we," Charlie offered as he placed a coffee in front of Quinn.

Busy stirring her coffee, Quinn didn't notice Mrs. Weller with Charlie walking around the other side of the table to the chairs directly across from herself and Darcy. Hearing them sit down, Quinn looked up from her coffee and was astonished at who was sitting in front of her. Actually, astonished was an understatement. Shocked and embarrassed were quite fitting given who she was sitting across from.

"Hello, Quinn. So good to see you again. I didn't realize you knew my brother."

THIRTY EIGHT

*A*t first Quinn had trouble speaking but then she awkwardly smiled and replied, "Sasha! And I didn't realize you were Darcy's sister." Quinn felt like a complete idiot and regretted every terrible thought she had had of Sasha and her yoga. She realized how much she had underestimated the woman who was at this very moment politely smiling at her with no animosity whatsoever.

Quinn just couldn't believe she was sitting across from 'yoga' Sasha. She was dressed in a very impressive business suit, was in complete control, so business-like.

I just can't wrap my head around Sasha being part owner of her own company, let alone a construction company. Who the hell is this family? Everyone's a 'big-wig'.

Darcy laughed and said, "I wanted to surprise you. When I told Sasha who the client was, she immediately knew who you were and asked me not to say anything."

"I'm sorry, Quinn. I knew it would come as a great surprise to you. After all, you really only know me from my yoga studio near the café, which is a side business for me, a guilty pleasure you might say. Weller Construction is my main job, the one that keeps food on the table. I can't rely on the yoga studio financially but I love it." Sasha explained. "I knew you would never make the connection because I've never used my last name at the studio."

"Sasha, I don't know what to say. I feel like I owe you an apology..." Quinn felt the need to explain her actions.

"There is no need, Quinn."

"If you ladies are done catching up, then I think we need to get down to business." Charlie convened the meeting and they began going over the contract, line by line.

After much discussion, questions asked and answered, it was time to sign the contract. Quinn suddenly grew nervous and hesitated momentarily.

"I want to reassure you, Quinn, that we will take the greatest of care while we renovate your cabin. Darcy has explained to both Charlie and myself, what it means to you and we will do everything we can to preserve all of the personal touches your grandparents put into the place. I promise you, it is in good hands with us."

Looking up at Sasha then over to Charlie, who nodded his approval, Quinn could see the sincerity in their eyes. Smiling, Quinn nodded and picked up the pen.

After all the papers were signed, Quinn looked at Darcy and said, "Well, I suppose there's no turning back now."

"Trust me, Sasha and Charlie's company is one of the best. You can't go wrong letting them do the work," Darcy offered.

"He's right, Quinn. We only hire the best people and we have very high standards. We will do a good job for you, we promise." Charlie was very sincere. Quinn could understand why clients do business with them. Both Sasha and Charlie were very professional with a strong air of competence about them.

"We want to thank you, Quinn, for allowing us this opportunity to expand our business in this way. We weren't sure what direction we wanted to go but when Darcy approached us with this opportunity, there was no hesitation on our part to move forward with it. It seemed like an excellent opportunity to expand our current business plan." Sasha smiled warmly, giving Quinn confidence that she had made the right decision.

Chapter THIRTY EIGHT

"I have complete faith in both of you." Quinn was quite truthful.

Wait until I tell François about this! He will fall over when he hears about Sasha.

• ● •

Sunday was a busy day at Dills and Dolls, the regulars were everywhere. Looking around the café, Quinn waved to François who was sitting at their usual table. Grabbing a latte and sitting down, Quinn couldn't wait to tell him about Sasha.

"Are you kidding me?!" François' jaw dropped. "Sasha?!"

"Yup!"

"Sasha? Who runs the yoga studio?" He was dumbfounded by the news.

"That's right!" Quinn laughed. "I was as shocked as you are, especially finding out she is Darcy's sister. What are the chances of that? Anyway, she and Charlie seem wonderful and I have faith that they can do the job. Lesson learned for both of us. You can't judge a book by its yoga pants or their annoying optimism."

"Well, I have to take another look at this lady. How can she be so well dressed and competent in the board room and such a hot mess in yoga pants…pardon the pun." François was bewildered by it all.

"I know!" Quinn was just as flabbergasted as François about it all. "Well, not about the yoga clothes. You and I can agree to disagree on those."

"Oh and we *do* disagree. So when will they start?"

"They need to get permits and some other prep work sorted out first but they are expecting to start in the Spring. Thinking for a moment Quinn added, "I'm so excited about all of this, François. My parents are going to be furious when they find out."

THIRTY NINE

*W*inter came and went and Spring arrived with a rainy vengeance. *April showers bring May flowers. Well, April is certainly showering down on us today.* Quinn frowned as she looked outside.

Hearing her mobile ring, Quinn ran to answer it and smiled to see that it was Darcy calling.

"Hi Quinn. I hear Charlie called you."

"Yes, I'm so excited. He said they will begin renovations by the end of the month and it was time to clean out the cabin. François and I will be heading up in the next week or two. The weather will hopefully be good by then and with any luck it won't take more than a day or two to get it done." Chuckling she added, "Of course, it will be the longest couple of days of my life listening to him complain the entire time."

Laughing, Darcy said, "Well, I'm going to meet up with Sasha and Charlie to discuss timelines this morning but how about dinner later? Are you free?"

"Sounds great! Come by my place and I'll cook." Quinn was happy that her relationship with Darcy had grown even closer over the winter. It was as if they had been in a relationship for much longer than they actually had and it felt right. It felt good to have finally put Spencer and their toxic relationship behind her.

Hanging up from Darcy, Quinn decided to head out to do some shopping. Quickly changing, she grabbed her purse and left. Walking through her lobby, she noticed that Mrs. Martin was talking to George, their concierge. As she got closer, Quinn tried not to laugh hearing their conversation.

"George, the taxi hasn't arrived. Where could it be?"

"Mrs. Martin, you never asked me to call you a taxi but I would be happy to do so."

"Really? I was sure I had, George. Are you sure I didn't ask you to call them for me?"

"Yes, quite sure, Mrs. Martin. No worries though, I will call now and they will be here shortly, I assure you."

Same old Mrs. Martin. Forgetful, yet sweet. She must drive George crazy though. He has such patience.

"Good morning, Ms. Fairchild. Have a lovely day. It looks like the rain has stopped for now," George called out as Quinn walked past.

"Thank you, George! Hello, Mrs. Martin." Quinn responded.

"Oh hello, Dear! You're looking rather lovely today." Mrs. Martin waved as she struggled to get seated in one of the chairs in the lobby.

"Thank you!" Quinn shouted to them collectively as she walked through the door to the now sunny, cool day that greeted her. The breeze was fresh, the sky clearing of the rain clouds. Spring was in the air.

Quinn decided she would head to Shore Street. It was the 'go to' street if you wanted to do any kind of decent shopping. Everyone knew that it was high-end and expensive and Quinn used to frequent it far more in her previous life than she ever would today. Her finances just didn't allow for it anymore but it didn't bother her quite as much as it used to. Today was different though. Today she was going to treat herself. To what? She hadn't decided just yet…but something.

The streets were very busy. Spring was evident everywhere. People were bustling around and wearing brightly coloured clothing. Quinn loved the energy in the air. She felt genuinely happy. Part of this was the lack of communication with her family for the last several months. That was enough to put a smile on her face alone, not to mention, knowing that the cabin was going to get fixed up. For the first time in a very long time she was excited for the future.

Admiring the neighbourhood that she had once frequented, it felt like she was seeing it for the first time. Looking up at Ocean's Jewellery, Quinn couldn't help but notice the new facade. *Lovely! They actually managed to modernize the old building.* Glancing around, she was looking across the street at Marcel's on Shore when she accidentally ran into someone.

"Oh, pardon me." Quinn said as she picked her purse up off the ground. Standing up again, she looked at the person who immediately squealed with fake delight.

"Quinn! Oh my God! Quinn Fairchild! How are you doing?!"

Are you kidding me? You couldn't let me just enjoy today?

"Mandy. Mandy Baker." Quinn was trying not to show that she was less than delighted with the encounter.

Mandy's family were members of the Emerald Country Club, the same club Quinn's family belonged to, and as much as their parents were good friends, Quinn had never been particularly fond of Mandy. She always found Mandy to be pretentious and at this moment Mandy was the last person Quinn wanted to see.

"Quinn Fairchild! How *are* you, Quinn? It's so great to see you again after…well…".

The awkwardness was evident, however, Quinn noticed that Mandy ignored it and continued.

"You look…well." Mandy forced the conversation.

Quinn frowned as she noticed Mandy checking her over, feigning sincerity.

"You also, Mandy."

I would love to be anywhere but right here, right now.

"I hear you are living in the theatre district. That's…nice…"

And the awkwardness continues.

"Yes, I've lived there for almost two years, Mandy. I'm surprised my parents didn't tell you that." She wasn't really surprised, she was purposely trying to make Mandy feel less than important thinking she wasn't privy to pertinent gossip about Quinn's life. It wasn't nice but she couldn't help herself.

"Yes, well…" Mandy cleared her throat and looked down.

Glancing at Mandy's left hand Quinn noticed a ring.

"Oh, you're engaged." Quinn desperately wanted to divert the attention away from herself.

Quickly tucking her hand into her coat pocket, Mandy uncomfortably replied, "Oh, yes. Yes, I am."

"That's wonderful!" Quinn faked it.

"Well, um…yeah." Mandy was clearly uncomfortable but then offered, "Would you like to see my ring?"

Not really.

"Oh, um, sure, okay." Quinn reluctantly agreed.

Mandy pulled her hand out and momentarily admired the shiny diamond on her finger before holding her hand out to show Quinn.

Looking at the ring, Quinn's heart felt like it stopped. She had trouble breathing. Tears immediately came to her eyes and she had trouble swallowing, let alone speaking.

Seeing the tears in Quinn's eyes, Mandy said, "I know. It's beautiful isn't it? Tears came to my eyes the first time I saw it as well. I absolutely love it. I've never seen anything so beautiful in all my life." Clearly Mandy's awkwardness had subsided as she spoke.

"Quinn? Are you alright?"

Quinn's head was spinning. She felt like she was going to faint.

"Oh." Trying to contain her emotions, Quinn added, "Yes, I'm...I'm fine. I just realized that I have an appointment that I'm late for. I'll have to go, Mandy."

"Of course. It was wonderful to see you, Quinn."

Quinn turned and walked away as quickly as possible. The last she heard was Mandy shouting after her, "Let's do lunch sometime."

Once out of range, Quinn ran and kept running until she reached a small park. Practically falling onto a bench, she tossed her purse beside her. It was only then that the tears began to stream and she sobbed uncontrollably. She couldn't stop crying. All of the years of emotion and heartache flooded out. She didn't care that people were walking by and staring. She didn't care that both her makeup and her nose were running.

I can't believe it! I thought I was past all of this.

It was as if the universe just knocked her down one more time except this time she didn't feel like getting back up again. She felt completely defeated.

Looking across the street, she realized she was in the park directly across from her condo. Grabbing her purse, she clutched it tightly in her hand as she quickly walked across the street, through the lobby, up the elevator and into her condo. Standing just inside her door, looking around, coat on and purse still clutched tightly she was slowly regaining her composure although she felt exhausted. Standing there thinking, she began to come to a realization that actually surprised her.

"Fuck this!"

Walking over, she picked up the phone and dialled an all too familiar number. She had one phone call to make and if she didn't do it now, she knew she wouldn't have the nerve to do it later.

"Hello?"

Hearing his voice, her nerves threatened to get the best of her but she took a deep breath and continued.

"Spencer?"

"Yes?" There was a moment of hesitation as he acknowledged who was calling him. "Quinn?"

"You fucking bastard! How could you give my engagement ring to Mandy?" She was livid.

"What? How do you even know and why do you even care? You're the one who chose to leave the relationship, not me. You've only got yourself to thank for this."

"You've got to be kidding!" Quinn couldn't believe what she was hearing.

"Listen Quinn, if you're calling to get back together, you can forget it. You lost your opportunity a long time ago, not to mention your dignity. You could have stayed and kept that ring for yourself but of course, not you, Quinn. Always thinking of yourself. How selfish can you be? Not for one minute did you consider how I felt, how humiliating it was for me to have to face everyone at the club after you left. So, yeah, I gave Mandy the ring. Why not? What was I to do with it? Wait for you to decide to come to your senses?"

"Me! Come to *my* senses? That's laughable. I *did* come to my senses when I decided to leave you!"

"And how is that working out for you, Quinn? My God, you've hit the proverbial bottom of the barrel haven't you? You're an emotional wreck. You have no job, no money, you sleep with every degenerate you meet. My God, you were even thrown in jail…" His words were intended to hurt.

"How…" Quinn couldn't believe what she was hearing.

"Yes, that's right. I know what's going on. Your mother and I speak." Thinking for a moment, Spencer added, "My God, you've changed. It's pathetic, really…" Spencer's voice was cold and emotionless.

Unable to hide the scorn in his voice he added, "I actually feel sorry for you. You used to have such class…"

Chapter THIRTY NINE

That was all Quinn needed to hear.

"Fuck you, Spencer! The best thing I ever did was to leave you. My God! You slept with every woman at the club who would give you the time of day, and then some! How dare you judge me you hypocritical bastard! Well, don't worry, I can assure you that I have absolutely no interest in getting back together with you. I have no regrets about leaving you." Before Spencer could speak again, Quinn added, "Oh, and Spencer?"

"Yes, Quinn?" Spencer sounded bored and completely uninterested in what she had to say next but she didn't care. She was saying what she needed to, once and for all.

"I would much rather spend my days sleeping around with every degenerate I meet, than ever having to spend another minute with you, you fucking asshole!"

The call didn't take long.

After hanging up, Quinn grabbed her keys, walked out of her condo and headed for her car.

FORTY

"**I** have no idea where she is. I've been at work all day and now I'm at Jorge's. Why do you ask?" François wondered.

"We were going to have dinner tonight and I've been trying to get her, but no answer." Darcy replied.

"Have you gone over to her place? Maybe she's not feeling well." François asked.

"Yes, I was there after work. She wasn't there." Darcy thought for a moment. "So, you haven't heard from her at all?"

"No, I haven't and now I'm quite concerned. The fact that she hasn't called all day and now it's almost eight o'clock makes me think something is seriously wrong." François became anxious. "You don't think she's been kidnapped do you?"

"No, I'm quite sure she hasn't been kidnapped, François." Darcy quietly chuckled to himself. "I'm sure there is a reasonable explanation. Let's wait until…" Darcy suddenly stopped.

"Until?" When Darcy said nothing, François' anxiety escalated. "You stopped talking. Why? Why?"

"Well, I'm just wondering, you don't think she could have gone to the cabin do you?" Darcy asked. "That's where she went the last time she was upset."

"You think she's upset about something? About what?" François' concern continued to grow.

"No, not really, just thinking out loud."

"She's never taken off without letting me know where she is going…" François wasn't sure whether to be worried or angry.

"Don't worry, François, I'm sure she's fine. Maybe she decided to go start packing up." Darcy tried to calm François, who was becoming increasingly upset.

"Well, I suppose she could have gone to the cabin but why wouldn't she have let *me* know…or you, for that matter? Besides, she promised me dinner at Pier 4 so I don't think she would…" Suddenly coming to a realization, François said, "You don't think she's gone to pack up so she doesn't have to pay for dinner at Pier 4 do you?" He was mulling over the possibility. "She better not be!" François was immediately indignant.

Laughing, Darcy said, "I'm sure she wouldn't renege on your deal, François."

"Well, none of it makes any sense to me. I think we should call the police, report her missing."

"No, we don't need to call the police and report her missing. She's barely been gone an afternoon. You need to relax, François. I'm sure she's fine." Darcy reasoned, "That's the only place she could have gone. I really think she went there." Darcy felt confident. "I'll try calling her again. If I don't get an answer, I'll take a drive out there."

"Okay, but that's an awful long way to drive when you aren't even sure she's there." Thinking for a moment, François got an idea. "Wait a minute! I can track her on my mobile. Well, track her cell phone. As long as her cell battery hasn't died that is. Besides, if she's been kidnapped it will help the police find her. One moment and let me grab my mobile, it's in my office."

Darcy shook his head in disbelief hearing what François just said. He had gotten used to François' dramatics over the last several months.

Within a few minutes, François returned to the phone.

"You were right! That's where she is! Thank God!" François was relieved.

Chapter FORTY

"Great thinking, François. So, now we know where she is, I'll head up in the morning to find out what's going on."

"Don't you think you should go tonight?"

"She's a big girl, François, she can take care of herself. She may need some time on her own and besides, it's late. I would have a hard time finding the place in the dark. I'll leave first thing in the morning," Darcy reassured.

"Well, let me know what's going on once you get there." François was relieved he didn't have to go but certainly would have if he thought his friend needed him.

FORTY ONE

The drive was long but arriving at the cabin the next morning, Darcy was relieved to see Quinn's car still in the driveway. The last thing he needed was to arrive, only to find out she left for home.

After knocking with no answer, Darcy opened the door and walked in. Calling out to Quinn with no response, he walked into the living room and noticed that the fireplace was still warm with embers. Chuckling when he saw that there were a couple of empty wine bottles knocked over on the floor with an empty glass sitting beside them, he picked them up.

Making his way down to the kitchen, he peeked into the two bedrooms as he walked by. Quinn's grandmother's bedroom had a messed up bed and clothes strewn across the floor but no Quinn. The guest room was neatly made up with no sign of use.

Once in the kitchen, Darcy placed the wine bottles and glass on the counter and looking around, noticed dirty dishes strewn around the kitchen and a couple of pots with leftover food in them on the stove. Calling out to Quinn again, Darcy heard nothing and decided to make his way outside.

Walking back out to the front of the cabin, he took a deep breath in, smelling the fresh scent of spring in the air. It was quite cool out and the sky was overcast. Deciding to go around to the back, Darcy shook his head as he rounded the corner. On the back porch was an old porch swing and laying in it, sound asleep, was Quinn wearing pyjamas, with her coat, hat, mitts and slippers on. She was wrapped in a blanket with a small, dirty pillow tucked under her head.

She must be freezing out here.

Quietly walking up to her, he hesitated to wake her up. She looked so peaceful. He didn't want to disturb her. Leaning in he kissed her on the forehead. When she didn't move, he went through the back door of the cabin, grabbed a warmer blanket and walking back out, covered her up with it. Sitting down in one of the Adirondack chairs on the porch, Darcy phoned François.

"What did she say? Why didn't she call?" François was no longer worried but grew angry with his friend. "You tell her I'm mad as hell that she didn't even let me know where she was."

Speaking quietly into the phone, Darcy said, "Will do, François. I'll call you later on."

Hanging up, Darcy went in to clean up the kitchen and make some coffee. Pouring himself a cup, he headed back outside and sat back down again.

Admiring the view, he had to admit, it was something he could get used to. He understood why Quinn loved it here so much. It was a nice reprieve from the city. There was still a little snow on the ground in the wooded areas. Listening to crows caw out in the distance, he smiled as he watched a couple of squirrels chasing each other down one tree, then up another. Trees were rustling in the wind. The forest of pine trees was picture perfect. He couldn't deny that it was relaxing here.

Hearing a moan, he looked over to see Quinn ever so slightly moving. After seeing the empty wine bottles, he knew to just let her sleep it off. There was no doubt her head would hurt. Resting his head back on the chair, he closed his eyes and just listened to Mother Nature at her best.

In the distance, he could hear thunder and opening his eyes was surprised to see dark clouds rolling in rather quickly. It wasn't long before the rain began and he was grateful for the covered porch. Soon the lightning was upon them and the rain grew heavier. Looking over to Quinn, he was amazed that she could actually sleep through it all.

Within minutes there was a bright flash of lightning followed by a deafening clap of thunder directly over the cabin and with that, Quinn awoke with a start. Not seeing Darcy there at first, she sat up and tightly wrapped the blanket around herself.

"Thought that clap of thunder might wake you up." Darcy said nonchalantly as he sipped on his coffee.

Screaming, Quinn fell off the swing and found herself sitting on the porch floor staring in shock at Darcy sitting there.

"What the hell?! What are you doing here? You scared me! " She was less than enthusiastic. The hangover didn't help much. Her headache was pulsating and she held her head with one hand to try and lessen the pain.

"Question really should be, what are *you* doing here?"

"What do you mean?" She asked defensively.

"Oh, I don't know. Considering you left town without uttering a word of your plans to myself or more importantly, to François. For all François knew, you could have been kidnapped and in the trunk of some pervert's car somewhere." He didn't believe that but offered it for dramatic effect and knew François would approve.

Sitting back up on the porch swing, Quinn stared out at the rain. "I'm fine and I don't answer to you...or François. Can I not come up to the cabin without having to make some grand announcement?"

"I suppose you can, yes."

She became haughty. "Yes, I should think so."

"Of course, he almost called the RCMP and filled out a missing person's report. I had to hold him back from that. It was all I could do to keep François from calling them in and setting up a manhunt."

Out of the corner of his eye he could see Quinn staring at him then look away. Glancing over he watched as she shook her head and rolled her eyes in disbelief.

"I assured him that you would never just leave without calling, without a perfectly good explanation of course, and that if you did, you would have been sure to let him know that you were fine. That you would never be so selfish as to leave your friend frantically wondering if you were dead in a ditch somewhere nor offer me dinner then leave town unannounced. That it would just be thoughtless of you…" Slowly taking a sip of his coffee, Darcy added, "…without a perfectly good explanation of course…"

Quinn once again looked his way then dropped her head down.

"Well…", she began.

"I assured him that when I saw you that you would most assuredly beg forgiveness for being so absolutely inconsiderate…"

"Okay, okay, I get it. I should have called." She was getting annoyed now. "I'm sorry. I actually forgot about our dinner."

"Don't say sorry to me. Call François and tell *him* that you're sorry. He was the one worried sick about you." Darcy replied.

"Okay, fine. I'll call him later." Quinn felt a little ashamed for not letting François know where she was and also forgetting about her dinner plans with Darcy. Of course, at the time, she wasn't exactly thinking clearly.

"No, you'll call him now." Darcy handed her his phone.

Annoyed, she grabbed the phone from his hand then dialled up François. For Darcy, it was satisfaction enough to hear François giving her proper hell. He really didn't need to say anything more, François said it all by the sound of the conversation from this end.

"Hi, François."

"Yes, I'm fine, but…"

"No, I just needed a break."

"I'll explain later."

"I know…I know I should have…"

Chapter FORTY ONE

"Yes, I know I was supposed to have dinner with Darcy…"

"I forgot…"

"I didn't mean to worry you…either of you…"

"Okay then! I'm sorry!"

"Yes, I mean it."

"Fine! Yes. I'm *very* sorry."

"*Very, very* sorry."

"I said…"

"François, I said I was sorry."

"Oh my God, François!"

"If you don't stop…"

"Okay then."

"What the hell is that supposed to mean?"

"I am *not* acting like a baby!"

"I am not!"

"Okay, enough, François!"

"Yes, I know you love me and yes, I love you too."

"Okay, yeah. Okay. I'll talk to you later."

Handing Darcy back his phone, Quinn said nothing.

"Was François upset?" Darcy antagonized her.

"Oh, shut the hell up!"

FORTY TWO

*A*fter dinner Quinn and Darcy sat in the living room with a fire roaring in front of them. She hated to admit it but she was actually glad Darcy came looking for her.

"So, why *did* you leave anyway?" Darcy wanted to know what was going on. "Second thoughts about renovating the cabin?"

"No, nothing like that."

Darcy said nothing, allowing Quinn some space. The room was very quiet for a few minutes before she started to open up.

"I just needed some time to decompress." Thinking for a moment, she added, "I over-reacted to something."

"Okay." Darcy was curious but respected her privacy.

Relaying the story of when she met up with Mandy, she finished, "…and that bastard, Spencer, had given her *my* engagement ring. The ring he gave me when he proposed. I know it sounds silly, but it hurt." Composing her thoughts she added, "It was like I wasn't important."

"You weren't." Darcy unemotionally offered.

"Well, thanks a lot! That's cold!" Quinn couldn't believe he just said that.

"I don't mean it to hurt you. It's just that he doesn't think anyone but himself is important. He never likely did and he never likely will. Sounds to me like you dodged a bullet when you left him, for more than one reason," he grinned. "After all, you ended up with me." Darcy winked at Quinn who immediately rolled her eyes.

"This is true. It really is too bad I drew the short straw," she teased.

"Hey! Hurtful." Darcy chuckled, happy to see Quinn really was fine.

"That's okay, I called him and told him what a piece of shit he really was."

Laughing, Darcy said, "He deserved that."

"Yup! I called him and told him what I thought of him."

"Good on you! And how did that make you feel?"

Laughing she added, "It made me feel pretty damn good!"

"I bet it did." Darcy smiled.

"Listen, I'm sorry, I shouldn't even be talking to you about this."

"I'm not that insecure, don't worry about it." Darcy reassured her.

Quinn looked at Darcy. Seeing that he genuinely meant what he said, she smiled and turned to look at the fire and sipped on her wine.

Darcy was the first to break the silence.

"So, does that mean you'll have sex with me tonight?" He was hoping the pillow she threw at him wasn't her final answer.

Getting up out of her chair, Quinn walked over to stand in front of Darcy. Slowly she began to unbutton her shirt. Removing it, she tossed it to the floor then removed her bra. Slowly removing her pants she tossed them aside with her shirt. Just as she was about to remove her panties, Darcy reached over and very slowly pulled them down for her. Closing her eyes, Quinn became almost breathless as she grew increasingly aroused by the gentleness and warmth of Darcy's lips as he began to tenderly kiss her body.

Slowly laying down onto the carpet in front of the roaring fire, Quinn kneeled over Darcy, then slowly lowered herself, kissing his soft lips as he simultaneously caressed her nipples with his fingers. The warmth of the fire heightened Quinn's entire physical being as she slowly and methodically kissed her way, inch by inch, down his muscular body.

Chapter FORTY TWO

Within moments, they rolled over, Darcy on top of Quinn. Catching her breath, Quinn felt him slowly slide inside of her. Placing her hands onto his firm buttocks Quinn was intoxicated by the feel of their bodies moving together, slowly, passionately, more intense with every movement in and then out. Acutely aroused, every inch of Quinn's body tingled as she moaned aloud with pleasure.

Moments later as they lay beside each other, breathless and enjoying this moment of ecstasy, Quinn smiled. She had never experienced anything as loving or passionate with Spencer and knew that she was where she now belonged.

FORTY THREE

*H*aving arrived home from the cabin the day before, Quinn headed to Dills and Dolls to meet up with François after work. Grabbing a latte, she sat down just as François arrived. Picking up his drink, François quickly headed to the table, sat down and wasted no time getting to the point.

"So, let's begin by saying, I forgive you for being such an inconsiderate pain in the ass."

"Are you kidding me?" Quinn shook her head. "Do we really need to go there again?"

"Oh, I think that we do." François said matter-of-factly.

Ignoring him, Quinn took a sip of her latte, glanced in the direction of the door and smiled when she saw Sasha entering. She had a renewed respect for the woman and vowed to go back to yoga and give it another try.

Waving, Quinn said, "There's Sasha." She was trying to deflect the conversation and it worked.

François looked over and immediately lost his patience. "Oh my God! That's it! Executive in her other life or not, that woman will never learn! I'll be right back."

François got up from his chair, then walked quickly towards the front of the café. Quinn shook her head in amazement at his lack of tolerance. Watching as he approached Sasha, Quinn couldn't take her eyes off her friend as he very animatedly spoke. *No doubt upset that she's still wearing those horrible workout clothes, as he puts it. He has such nerve.*

François was very excitedly using his hands to point out whatever it was about Sasha's clothes that he clearly had an issue with. He was pointing out the waist, her legs, ankles. *Jeez, how much more could he possibly point out?* It wasn't long before she had the answer to her question. *Ah, I see, clearly the top was too loose or something. Nope, I think it's the colour. Nope. Not sure what that's all about.*

She chuckled watching him spin Sasha around then put his hands on his waist in frustration. Sasha was looking completely overwhelmed but Quinn didn't feel sorry for her. She knew what she was getting into the moment she walked through those doors, knowing François could be here to assess her clothing at any given time.

Sasha shook her head no, then nodded. Finally, looking over at Quinn, she waved and left.

Clearly finished with Sasha, François walked back, sat back down across from Quinn and let out a very exasperated sigh.

"Had a problem with what Sasha was wearing, did you?"

Rolling his eyes, François shook his head and said, "She's coming to my shop tomorrow. I can't take it anymore, Q! That woman looks like some poor Cinderella version of a business owner."

"But it's yoga."

"And she's the owner," François baulked. "If she can dress for the board room, she can dress for yoga."

"But still, a yoga instructor who needs to wear yoga clothes. Besides, you don't even design yoga clothes." Quinn tried to get through to François.

"Well, I do now," he muttered, sipping on his latte then quickly smiled as Jorge approached their table.

"Hi François. Quinn." Jorge never took his eyes off François as he spoke. "Can I get you another latte?"

Chapter FORTY THREE

"No thanks." Quinn knew he hadn't heard her. Just then her mobile rang. Answering it, she wasn't long hanging up and squealing with excitement. Jorge had left and François jumped from the unexpected noise.

"Guess what?!"

"What?"

"Darcy just called and Sasha and Charlie can start the renos sooner than expected. I'm surprised Sasha didn't come over to tell me when she was here."

"Actually, she wanted to but…"

"But you took up all of her time," Quinn finished.

"Yes, well, first things first. Anyway, that's great about the cabin! When are they starting?" François was genuinely happy for his friend.

"Next week." Quinn could hardly wait for them to start.

"So I guess that means we have to go and clean things out this weekend." His lack of enthusiasm was very evident.

"Yup! And I bet you can't wait! We will go up Thursday morning so you will have to take a couple of days off work. That way we can be done by Saturday or Sunday." Quinn laughed.

"Yeah, yeah, yeah. If it wasn't for dinner at Pier 4 with Jorge…" François reminded.

"Yes, I know. You wouldn't even be doing this. I get it." Quinn rolled her eyes.

FORTY FOUR

ater that week, Quinn was relieved to finally arrive at the cabin. It had been the longest drive she had ever experienced. François had whined all the way. If he wasn't hungry, he was thirsty, and if it wasn't that, the drive was too long or her car wasn't as comfortable as his. It was exhausting and she'd had enough. Pulling up, she couldn't get out of the car fast enough. Grabbing her overnight bag from the backseat, she slammed the door shut, smiling at the sound of the echo it made as she momentarily reminisced.

"Oh my God! We finally made it!" François almost exploded as he got out of the car. "I didn't think we would ever get here!"

Ignoring him, Quinn walked up and opened the front door, hesitating before entering. She felt a tug at her heart. *I'll never get used to this.* The moment quickly passed when she felt a nudge from behind her.

"Okay, so let's get this party started. The sooner we pack up the sooner we can leave for civilization again," François ordered as he pushed past Quinn.

Following him in, Quinn tossed her bag onto the floor in the front hall.

The smell of cedar and pine was one of her favourite parts of coming back to the cabin. She made a mental note to remind Darcy once again that the kitchen cupboards and cedar walls in the living room were to remain. Her grandfather made all of those and she wasn't about to change them, no matter what design recommendations were made.

• ● •

Several hours later, Quinn could hear François shout from the living room something about being hungry, slave labour and being desperate for some wine. Standing in the entrance of the living room, leaning against the wall, arms crossed, Quinn stared at him until he noticed her.

"Oh, you heard that did you?" Knowing full well it was his intention all along.

"Slave labour?" She shook her head. "What are you? A child?" Dropping her arms, she turned and walked towards the kitchen, shouting back, "I'm making lunch and I don't want any complaints about what I make."

Dropping the packing tape he had in his hand, François immediately headed to the kitchen.

"Well, it's about bloody time! I'm starving!" Grabbing wine out of the fridge, François asked, "Want a glass?"

Nodding, Quinn gratefully accepted his offer.

Sitting down at the kitchen table, François asked, "So, what's for lunch?"

"Chili, salad and garlic bread."

"Homemade chili?"

"No, not homemade chili." Shaking her head she offered him a bowl. "It's from Bruno's."

"Bruno's? Well, now you've got my attention." François sat right up, eager for the food he was about to eat.

• ● •

The afternoon flew by and Quinn once again heard François holler from the living room, this time, that he was almost done packing up. She was feeling relieved because as much as she wanted everything to remain the same, she was getting excited about fixing the place up and hoped her grandmother would have been pleased. Her heart sank at the thought of her grandmother. There was a black hole in her life that would take a long time to heal, if it ever did. Quinn knew she hadn't completely come to terms with the loss.

Walking into the kitchen, Quinn stood still and looked around. She was suddenly feeling very tired.

"François!" She called out.

"Yeah?" he answered as he walked into the kitchen carrying boxes, tape and packing material. "What's up?"

"Let's stop and take a break for tonight. This has taken far less time than I thought it would. We only have the kitchen left and it won't take long. We can do it in the morning and I could really use a break." Sighing heavily, she added, "I'm tired."

François looked at his friend and realized that it must be emotionally draining for her and took pity.

"Sure. I could use a break…and some wine." Emptying his handful of packing materials down onto the kitchen table, he added, "And food."

Grabbing a bottle of red wine, glasses, some cheese and crackers, they headed back to the living room. Quinn grabbed some wood and started a fire in the fireplace while François poured the wine. Once the fire was roaring away Quinn settled into an easy chair and closed her eyes. Within moments she could hear snoring and looked over at François and smiled. She was enjoying the peaceful moment with the warm fire, wine and even listening to her friend snoring. It all just felt perfect.

FORTY FIVE

The next morning, Quinn had a hard time dragging herself out of bed. She knew that if she didn't get up to make breakfast that François wouldn't. The only things he hated more than the countryside, were cooking and getting up early.

Trudging down the hall in her pyjamas and bunny slippers, Quinn felt chilled. It was a cooler morning. Reaching the kitchen, she put the coffee on and filled the kettle up to boil for tea.

Opening the cupboard door, she became teary-eyed seeing the tea container on the shelf. About to grab it, she heard François come into the kitchen and closed the cupboard door so she could see him.

"Wow! You look like shit," she laughed.

"Fuck you, Q." He muttered sleepily. "What's for breakfast?"

"With that attitude, nothing."

"Yeah, okay. Well, I'm not in the mood for attitude from you either right now."

"Aren't we a bit cranky this morning?"

"I just want food and a coffee, then I might consider civil conversation."

"Coffee and food coming right up!"

• ● •

"That was actually quite delicious. I didn't realize that I could like a… what did you call that?"

"A toasted western sandwich," Quinn responded with some sarcasm which François didn't notice or ignored, she wasn't sure which. "I've only made it for you many times before."

"Oh, well, it was good." Sipping on his coffee he asked, "Did I like it before?"

Shaking her head in amazement, Quinn rolled her eyes and finished eating.

"So what do we have to do now? Just the kitchen?" François looked around the room.

"Yup, that's it! We should be able to head back later this afternoon. I honestly thought it would take a few days." Quinn was pleased. "Hey listen, why don't you go pack up your things and I'll clean up the dirty dishes in here and then we can go for a walk before we finish packing and leave. I think we could both use some fresh air and exercise."

"Yeah, I don't think so. What part of I don't like nature or the country don't you understand?"

"Okay but you're missing out on a beautiful day."

"Yeah, I'm devastated about that." François said unenthusiastically.

After cleaning up the kitchen, Quinn threw her sneakers and jacket on, grabbed her phone and headed out for a walk. Heading to the lake, she looked forward to a bit of thinking time and took in a deep breath of the crisp, fresh air.

● ● ●

Seeing Quinn trying to call him yet again, François sighed and answered the call.

"What?!" He didn't even try to hide his annoyance.

Chapter FORTY FIVE

"François! I've tried calling you a half a dozen times!" Quinn was frantic.

"I was on the phone with Jorge. What's so damn important that you need to interrupt my call, anyway?" François was impatient.

"I need help."

"Okay, sure, with what and where are you?" François was curious what she could possibly need help with on her walk.

"I'm stuck down by the lake. I need help."

"Really? Why? What happened?"

"Never mind that, just come now." Quinn was frantic. "Just follow the path down to the lake."

"Okay, okay."

● ● ●

Impatiently pushing aside some tree branches that were in his way, François shouted out for his friend.

"Quinn? Quinn? Where are you?"

"François?!"

"Where the hell are you?"

"Over here!"

Heading in the direction of Quinn's voice, François pushed through some brush that lead him to the beach and once through, immediately began to laugh.

FORTY SIX

"Stop laughing! It's not funny!"

"Oh, this is too good not to laugh about and yes, it is funny!" He was almost choking on his laughter as he spoke. "Seriously, I can't even imagine how you got there."

"Just get me down from here."

Quinn was hanging upside down from a large tree branch that hung out over the water. Wrapped around her right ankle was a thick rope that clearly became entangled and left her dangling back and forth in the wind.

"Now!" Quinn shouted.

Laughing, François said, "Hold on! Let me get a picture of this. This is just too precious not to capture."

"Don't be an ass! Get me down!"

"No, no really, I need to take a pic. One sec." François knew he was antagonizing her but he couldn't help himself.

"Are you kidding me?" Quinn was trying to spin herself around to see him.

After taking the picture, François asked, "How in hell did you get up there like that?" He was mentally trying to figure out the best strategy to get her down.

Sighing, Quinn could feel her foot getting more numb by the minute. "I climbed up here and thought I would pull the rope back towards the beach so it could be easily reached. But I kept dropping it, so, I finally got the brainwave to wrap it around my ankle so I wouldn't lose it as I crawled back along the branch."

The wind was picking up and Quinn felt herself swinging faster and starting to spin around even more than she already had been. She was having difficulty trying to look and see what François was doing.

"Trouble was, that I lost my balance and fell off the branch and well, the rest is pretty much self explanatory." The blood had rushed to her head long ago and she was feeling dizzy.

Hearing nothing, she called out, "What the hell are you doing?"

"Don't be so impatient, I'm coming."

"Wait! Here, grab my phone just in case it falls in the water." Throwing her phone to François he carefully zipped it up into his sweater pocket.

So, what's your plan?" Quinn called out.

"I have no idea. I'm just trying to figure out how to climb this fucking tree." François stood staring up at the tree unsure of what to do next.

"Are you kidding me? Just climb the damn tree!"

"Well, that's easy for you to say but I've never climbed a tree before," François hollered back.

"What? What do you mean, you've never climbed a tree before?" Quinn couldn't believe what she was hearing. "You've *never* climbed a tree, EVER?"

"Nooo, I've never climbed a tree, EVER." François mocked her.

Quinn was losing her patience and felt that she would most likely lose consciousness if she hung upside down much longer. *I really should have taken Sasha's yoga classes, maybe I could have pulled myself up the rope and out of this ridiculous situation.*

"Well, whatever you do, hurry up for heaven's sake!" she shouted.

"Yeah, yeah, yeah! Just shut the hell up!" François too was losing his patience.

Chapter FORTY SIX

There was a moment's silence when all Quinn could hear were grunts and cursing.

"Who hasn't climbed a tree before? What kind of sheltered childhood did you have?"

Quinn tried to look around to get a look at what was going on but only managed to make herself spin faster, with help from the wind. "Geez, François, hurry up!" She shouted.

"Just shut the fuck up, Q!"

It took him several minutes to climb the tree and reach the branch that Quinn was hanging from.

Feeling tugs on the rope, Quinn was relieved when François finally made it to the rope.

"How the fuck am I supposed to undo this?" He yelled down to her.

"It's not knotted, just wrapped, so find the other end, unwrap it, then pull me up."

"Are you kidding me? How the hell am I supposed to pull you up?"

"Okay well, maybe loosen it and slide it along the branch till I'm over the ground and then slowly lower me down." Quinn was having trouble thinking clearly after hanging upside down for over an hour at this point.

"Q?"

"Yeah?"

"How deep is the water below you?" François called out.

"Maybe ten feet or so. I dunno, why do…" Screaming, Quinn disappeared into the water. Seconds later she scrambled to get her head above the very cold water, spitting it out of her mouth before swimming to shore.

"What the fuck, François!" Coughing, Quinn crawled onto the beach then laid back staring up at the sky. "Why did you do that? It's bloody freezing! I could get hypothermia."

It was a few minutes before François gingerly made his way back down from the tree, walked over and stood staring down at his friend.

"Oh I don't know. Maybe because I couldn't have dragged your sorry ass along that tree to the shore. Did you honestly think I could?"

"You're an asshole, you know that?" She mumbled. Once her head felt clear she sat up and unwound the rope from her ankle.

François offered his hand to help her stand. By now, Quinn was visibly shaking from the cold. Removing his sweater, he handed it to her to put on.

"Let's get back to the cabin so you can warm up. That is, unless you want to do some more swimming," he teased.

Ignoring him, Quinn playfully smacked his arm.

Walking along, François added, "You know you're lucky that's not one of my cashmere sweaters or I wouldn't have been able to let you wear it while you're wet."

"Yeah, I know." Quinn replied knowing her friend wasn't kidding.

FORTY SEVEN

*A*rriving back at the cabin, François went to finish packing up his overnight bag while Quinn changed into dry clothes. Heading into the kitchen, she put the kettle on to boil. She was cold and needed something to warm up.

Hearing François in the washroom, Quinn started to empty all the food from the fridge into a cooler. Hearing the kettle boil, she looked for the herbal tea she had brought with her from a previous visit but the box was now empty. Reluctantly, she opened up the cupboard but smiled when she saw the tea container. It was metal with a floral pattern all over it. She had been quite young when she gave it to her grandmother for a birthday gift. Her grandmother told her how much she loved it and had used it ever since. The sweet memory brought tears to Quinn's eyes. Reaching in, she pulled it out. About to shut the cupboard door, Quinn noticed an envelope on the shelf behind where the container had been sitting. Picking it up, she took a quick breath in, suddenly feeling weak. Her name was written on the envelope in her grandmother's handwriting.

Sliding down the cupboards, Quinn sat on the floor, knees bent. Placing the tea container on the floor beside her, Quinn's hands shook as she carefully opened the envelope. Pulling out the letter that was inside she began reading.

Quinn Dear,

I wrote this letter and have provided my lawyer, Mr. Foster, with a copy. I hid it behind the tea tin because, well, you

245

know that family of ours, I didn't want it publicized with my will, and with your love of tea I knew you would find it eventually, Dear.

By now my will has been read and you have been told that I have left the cabin and all of its contents, which includes this letter, to you. I know how much you love being here, likely as much as your grandfather and I did. So this is the bottom line…it's going to cost a lot of money to fix this place up and maintain it. I know this and I know you can't afford it. After your grandfather died I was tired, Dear, and had no desire to change anything. We had been investing our money over the years so I decided to pull some of our investments and open up a bank account in your name, hoping that once I was gone you would use it to renovate this old place.

I love you, Dear, your grandfather loved you and I couldn't think of a better person to give this cabin to. Make it your own home now, Quinn. You exceeded all of our expectations. We were both so very proud of you. Please don't be sad. Live your life to the fullest, don't waste a moment.

I love you, Quinn. You will always be my sweet angel. Remember, that life goes on, Quinn, Dear, but I will always be with you.

Love Grandma
XO

Quinn was sobbing and could barely read the letter through her tears. Shaking off the questions she had, Quinn wiped the tears from her face with the sleeve of her sweater.

I really must learn to carry tissue.

Picking up the bankbook that had been enclosed, she slowly opened it.

Chapter FORTY SEVEN

"Oh my God!" she shouted as she dropped the book onto the floor.

She had stopped crying and just sat there stunned, staring at the bankbook lying in front of her. Finally, picking it up again, she slowly opened it once more. Shocked, she couldn't believe what she was seeing. It was surreal.

Screaming, she struggled to stand but lost her footing. François came running into the kitchen.

"What's wrong?! What's happening?!"

She couldn't speak and kept staring at the bankbook.

"Q! What's wrong? Why did you scream?" The suspense was killing him.

She still couldn't speak. Looking up at François she tried handing him the bankbook but it slipped out of her hand onto the floor.

"You okay, Q?"

She just stared at François.

Confused, François picked up the bankbook and proceeded to open it. "What's all the fuss….Holy fucking shit!" he screamed out. His mouth dropped open as he stared at the information before him.

By now Quinn was standing but felt weak and shaky. "I know, right?" She was trying to gather her thoughts. "I just can't believe it. Listen to this." Reading the letter out to François, they stood in silence. Quinn took back the bankbook and opened it once again, wanting to be sure it wasn't all a dream.

"Wow, Q. Is this for fucking real?" François was dumbfounded.

"Yeah…I guess it is. I dunno. I'm not sure." She wanted to believe it but wasn't completely confident that it wasn't just a cruel joke. *But who would do something like that? Certainly not Grandma and I'm sure no one else has been to the cabin since she died.*

"Do you realize what this means, Quinn?"

Suddenly looking at her friend, she became immediately concerned.

"No. What does it mean?" She asked cautiously, unsure of what he was getting at.

"Q, there's a shit load of money in this account! That's a six figure bottom line right there! You're rich!" He was hoping she would grasp the significance of the situation. "Don't you get it? You're fucking rich!" François yelled.

"I'm rich? I have money?" Quietly talking to herself, Quinn was having a hard time comprehending it all.

Looking up at her friend, realization suddenly set in and she screamed, "Oh my God, François! I have money!" Grabbing and hugging him, she jumped up and down with him in her arms.

"I'm rich! I'm rich!"

Suddenly stopping, her smile slowly faded away.

"What's wrong?" François became concerned.

Her mind was racing. *What do I do with this? What if my parents decide they want to fight me for it? What if…*

"Q? What's wrong?"

"François, what if this isn't really for me?"

"That makes no sense, Q. The letter clearly states it's for you."

"But there's no date on it."

"So what!" François wasn't understanding her thinking.

"Maybe this was from years ago and the account is empty now. Or if there is money there what if it isn't intended for me? Maybe it's for my parents. Maybe it's a cruel joke." She became suddenly anxious.

"That's ridiculous! Clearly this is intended for you and if you look at the bank book, the last of the money was deposited…". Picking the book back up, François opened it and flipped to the last entry. "Okay…so the last deposit was made almost six months ago but that doesn't mean it's not there and it doesn't mean it's not meant for you."

"Oh my God! What if she withdrew the money after that? What if she had forgotten about this letter and the bank book? What if she changed her mind and there is nothing there?" Panic was setting in.

"François, what if…"

"You can easily find out, Quinn. It's Friday, the bank is still open. Just go and update the bank book."

Quickly looking up at her friend, Quinn said, "You're right! Why didn't I think of that? Let's go!"

Running down the hall, Quinn grabbed her purse and waved for François to hurry up.

"I'm coming, I'm coming!" He hated being rushed along.

Running outside to her car, Quinn quickly got in and started it, impatiently waiting for François.

"Geez, François! Hurry up!" She shouted out the window.

"Aren't you forgetting something?" François was just standing in the doorway of the cabin staring in her direction.

"What?! What?! Let's go!" She was losing her patience.

"Perhaps you should change."

"Wha…?" Looking down she realized she was still in her torn, stained track pants and slippers. "Oh crap!" Opening the car door, she ran back into the cabin, quickly got changed and ran back to the car, this time with her friend following close behind.

Driving into town, Quinn spotted the bank and parked nearby. Trying to keep her emotions in check, she was finding it hard not to be nervous. She could feel her hands shaking as she handed the teller the bank book.

"Hi…um…" she began. Taking in a deep breath, she continued, "…um…could you…could you update this for me please?"

"Absolutely. One moment." The teller took the book and walked over to the printer and placed the book into the machine. Walking back to her station, she quickly punched in something and Quinn could see the book starting to print. It was done in just a few seconds but it wasn't quick enough for Quinn.

The teller then walked back, retrieved the book, closed it and handed it back to Quinn.

"Is there anything else I can do for you today?" She asked.

"No…thank you." Quinn didn't want to open the book up for fear of her reaction. She anxiously looked at François and headed out the front door to her car with him following close behind. Sitting in the car, Quinn sat staring at the bank book while she waited for François to get in the car and shut his door.

"What if it says zero balance, François? What then?" Quinn was more nervous than she had ever been in her life.

Thinking for a moment, François calmly replied, "Well, Sweetheart, then you are no worse off than you were this morning when you got up. You aren't losing a thing."

Nodding her head in acknowledgement, Quinn said, "Maybe we should wait until we get back to the cabin. I'm too scared to look now."

The drive back was painstakingly slow. Walking into the cabin, Quinn headed straight to the kitchen and sat down at the table. François followed. Looking up at her friend Quinn took a deep breath in and then out again. Hands shaking, she slowly opened the book and turned to the last page. Looking at the final entry she closed it again, tears came to her eyes. She couldn't speak. She just handed the book to François.

Quickly opening the book up, François closed it again and looked at his friend as she sat there crying.

FORTY EIGHT

"**H**oly shit, Q! There's even more money in the account than there was before, from the interest alone!"

Quinn was having a hard time coming to terms with this news.

"Quinn! Aren't you happy?" François was confused by her silence.

Looking up she slowly smiled.

"Q?" François waited for her to say something, anything. Moments later he got his answer.

"Holy crap, François! I'm rich! I'm fucking rich!"

"What are you going to do?"

"I don't know!" She squealed. "What do you think I should do?"

"Well, you can't quit your job. You don't have one!"

"I don't believe it. It's like a dream."

"Well, if it's a dream then it's one fucking awesome dream!" François couldn't hold back his excitement.

"My God, François. I could buy a car!"

"Yeah, a really awesome car!"

"Or get a new place." Her mind was racing.

"A really awesome place!" François added.

"Or a whole new wardrobe!" She was getting more excited at the possibilities.

Stopping, François looked at his friend very seriously and insisted, "A really awesome wardrobe from F&F Fashions…"

Looking at him, she replied, "Yeah, I don't think so."

"And why not?"

"Your clothes are too ex-pen-sive!"

Rolling his eyes, François responded sheepishly, "Well…you can afford it now…"

Thinking for a moment, Quinn smiled, "Yay! I can afford things! Oh my God, I can pay for my own bail now!"

FORTY NINE

*T*he next day, Quinn sat in Mr. Foster's office, patiently awaiting his arrival. It wasn't long before he was sitting in his chair across the desk from her.

"So, Miss Fairchild, what can I do to help you?"

Clearing her throat, Quinn was nervous.

"Well, Mr. Foster. I just wanted to clarify something you said during the reading of my grandmother's will. Well, it was to me, after my parents and sister left."

"Certainly, what is it?"

"You said that the cabin and everything in it belonged to me now. Is that correct?" Quinn needed reassurance. She needed to hear it again.

"Yes, that is correct. That is exactly what your grandmother stated to me word for word. In fact, she insisted I write it down, exactly."

"So, *everything*...correct?"

"Yes."

"Every...last...thing in that cabin belongs to me and is beyond dispute. Correct?"

"Yes, Miss Fairchild. Is there a reason why you are asking?" Mr. Foster was curious.

"Well, I was cleaning out cupboards in the kitchen and I found this." Sliding the envelope over to Mr. Foster, he picked it up.

Removing the contents of the envelope, Mr. Foster read the letter first then opened up the bank book and looked it over. Closing it up, he carefully placed them both back into the envelope and slid it back across his desk to Quinn.

"Yes, it's all yours." He smiled as he calmly spoke.

"But there's over $765,000 dollars in that account. Are you sure?" Quinn was in disbelief. "*All* of it?"

"*All* of it." Mr. Foster responded. Removing his glasses he leaned back in his chair crossing his arms.

"Quinn, I am fully aware of this letter and the bank account. I wasn't aware as to how much your grandmother had in the account but I was quite aware that she was putting money away for you. She was very clear about what her intentions were but was insistent I not tell you about it. She wanted you to find it for yourself. She wanted it to be one last gift to you, from her."

"Really?" Quinn almost whispered as she began to cry.

"Really." Mr. Foster smiled and waited a moment before continuing. "If you will allow me a moment of unprofessionalism…off the record."

Quinn looked at him with curiosity and said, "Yes, of course."

"Your grandmother wasn't fond of your parents, or your sister for that matter, and she was quite clear about that with me. She had very definite ideas and I can assure you she didn't want the rest of your family to have this money. She loved you all but she *liked* you more than all of them combined, her words, not mine." He smiled kindly before continuing.

"They never treated her well and she wasn't blind to that fact. She often said they were condescending and quite frankly didn't give a damn about what she wanted." Smiling, he added, "She always spoke very highly of you, Quinn. She loved you very much."

"Oh," was all she could muster, her emotions raw.

"If I may, Quinn. You had a wonderful relationship with your grandmother. I would recommend you run with this, enjoy it. Don't share a penny with your family, they have enough. Use it to fix up that cabin, use it to make your life better. That's what Esther wanted for you."

Smiling, he was sympathetic to Quinn's position. He was aware how hard it was to come to terms with everything.

"Esther was a wonderful lady. We developed a nice friendship over the years. I miss her a great deal. I knew her well enough to say that she meant what she said in her letter to you. She would want you to go and enjoy your life, Quinn. Do that for your grandmother." Mr. Foster gave a heartwarming smile and stood up from his chair. Walking around his desk, he helped Quinn stand. Tears were rolling down her cheeks.

"Do you mind if I give you a hug, my dear?"

Quinn could only nod.

Hugging her, Mr. Foster pulled away and said, "Now wipe those tears away. Go and be happy. I'm here if you require any legal assistance or advice. It would be my pleasure to serve you as I did your grandmother for so many years."

Walking towards the door, Quinn stopped and turned around.

"Mr. Foster?"

"Yes, my dear?"

Biting down on her lip, she could barely speak.

"Thank you. Thank you for being there for my grandmother and thank you for your kind words. They mean a great deal to me."

"Of course, my dear." Mr. Foster smiled.

FIFTY

Standing outside of Mr. Foster's office, Quinn acknowledged to herself that she was content with the life she was living but could only now recognize just how much time she had wasted mourning the loss of her relationship with Spencer and trying to please her parents. She felt like the weight of the world had been removed and was instantaneously replaced by genuine happiness. She could appreciate more than ever having had her grandmother in her life, the cabin, and now Darcy, the money. *And yes, even François*, she chuckled to herself.

Walking out onto the front step of the building she was blinded by the sun. It had been raining when she went inside and she now needed to adjust to the sunlight. Stopping and smiling, she looked up to the sky and said aloud, "Grandma, you sure do know how to surprise a girl!"

Looking back down again, she spotted Darcy on the opposite side of the street leaning against his car, feet crossed at the ankles, arms crossed, smiling in her direction. Waving at him, Quinn quickly crossed the busy road, walked up to him and passionately kissed him, leaving him momentarily speechless. Her happiness unmistakable.

"How did you know where I was?" Thinking for a moment, she added, "Oh, right. François."

Clearing his throat, Darcy said, "François was rather evasive but I'm told you have something to celebrate?"

"That I do." She was excited to share her news with Darcy. "I've got plenty to celebrate and I'm just now realizing how much."

Thinking for a moment, tears came to her eyes. Looking back up to the sky, she whispered, "Thank you."